RANGER LOYALTY

BROTHERHOOD PROTECTORS WORLD

LAYLA CHASE

Twisted Page Press LLC

BROTHERHOOD PROTECTORS

ORIGINAL SERIES BY ELLE JAMES

CHAPTER 1

THE FIRST WARM breeze he'd felt this month rolled in from the south. Tag Redmond strolled along the sidewalk in downtown Butte, Montana, pausing at the next intersection. From the corner of his left eye, he watched without letting on until both Beagles sat at the end of the yoked leash. He waited two seconds then leaned down and scratched under their chins. "Good job, girls."

Today's therapy dog lesson emphasized walking with a loose leash among crowds. The population of Eagle Rock, his newly adopted hometown, was too small to provide a sufficient number of pedestrians. When the traffic light changed to green, Tag crooked his fingers, palm up. "Taffy, Pixie, heel."

He caught a couple amused glances on the faces of people walking toward him. The sight of a six-foot-two-inch cowboy, complete with straw Stetson, tethered to a pair of dogs only a foot high at the shoulders must be comical. After a glance in an adjacent window, he couldn't hold back a chuckle.

Memories rolled through his mind of places he'd visited less than a year earlier. Working with his K-9 buddy, Dex, in the Afghanistan desert provided immediate rewards. Their job had been to conduct explosives scent training, as well as instructing the locals on security methods. The Belgian Malinois was the smartest dog he'd been assigned in his eight-year career. He missed those sessions when Dex walked in the narrow space between his knees, maintaining an exact pace, as Tag, with his rifle held at shoulder height, demonstrated the method for the human-canine team to clear an area.

An ache stabbed the inside of his left thigh where he'd lost a fist-sized chunk of muscle from a firefight—almost as if the memory conjured the pain. Last year's injury resulted in a medical discharge from his Army Ranger unit. Thankfully, he'd recovered enough, and after hours of physical therapy, to walk with a normal gait.

A screech of tires brought him back to the present. Stiffening, he stopped, his boots scraping on the concrete. His heart rate rocketed, senses alert for encroaching danger. No whine of an incoming mortar or the sharp ratchet of a weapon being cocked sounded. After a moment filled with everyday noises and movements, he focused on his surroundings—city block, street signs, solid buildings, ambling pedestrians. Seeing no evident threat allowed him to draw in an even breath.

Taffy kept moving forward, pulling along a stiff-legged Pixie.

"Heel." Tag walked the pair to the right, took two steps, circled, and then stopped again. This time, they complied. He praised them both, tossing them a bit of freeze-dried chicken. Adjusting to life after serving in the Army proved challenging. Thankfully, his strong back and honed muscles were always appreciated on the family's cattle ranch in Wyoming. Those three months of riding the range, herding steers, and doing ranch chores had been essential, allowing him to set a new routine and work through the worst of his lingering nightmares.

Working with a couple of his mom's friends to help break their pets of bad habits seemed a natural extension of his expertise. One day, his mom handed him a book about therapy dogs and the good they did for hospital patients and people in assisted-living situations. A light went off over his head—he could use his acquired dog handler skills and teach the ones appropriate to civilian life. Even if that choice meant working with animals a fifth the size of what he was used to.

In a catching-up phone call with a Ranger

buddy, Rhys Morgan, Tag learned about the Brotherhood Protectors, a private security firm operated by ex-SEAL Hank Patterson. Within the week, he left the family ranch, drove north to Montana, and rented a five-acre place that abutted the Lewis and Clark National Forest. Working security would be an opportunity to use his skills and offer protection to those who needed it. An attitude ingrained into his psyche during his years of military service.

Before the next corner, he stopped shy of the entrance to First Pioneer Bank, pulled cloth tabs from his left back pocket, and crouched. "All right, ladies. Here's a chance to work on your indoor manners." Seeing their bright eyes focused on his face and their flop ears pointed forward, listening to his words, brought a smile. Both dogs wore a red vest imprinted with "therapy dog in training." Unfortunately, that label didn't always stop people from reaching out to touch them. Now, he attached tabs stating "do not pet" before going into businesses. He tugged the leash loop over his wrist.

Standing, he spotted a blonde approaching from about ten feet away. Wavy hair flowed behind her shoulders with each step. His pulse kicked up. He slid down his aviators an inch for a better look. Confidence exuded from her easy gait. Her lemon-yellow top clung to her curves in all the right places. A floral skirt swished around toned calves. Lace-trimmed socks peeked from the top of ankle boots. At least the woman wore heels of a sensible height, no more than two inches tall. So much smarter than the five-inch spikes he'd seen some women teetering on. They'd never get anywhere fast in an emergency. He stepped to the bank door, held it open with the tip of his boot, and tapped a finger to the brim of his hat. "After you, ma'am."

Her eyes rounded, and she dipped her chin. After a quick glance at the dogs watching with big brown eyes, she smiled. "Thank you."

The scent of citrus followed her. Tag grabbed the handle, ready to walk through and maybe find a reason to speak to this beauty again. Movement reflected in the bank's left-side glass door caught his attention.

A black, king-cab truck rolled unhurried in the nearby lane heading south—much slower than the posted speed limit.

Something about the crawling movement, and the intensity of the male passenger staring through the opened window at the bank entrance, lifted the hairs on the back of Tag's neck. His whole body tightened. Blood pounded in his ears, and he narrowed his eyes, looking for the glint of sunlight off metal. He flashed back to times in the sandbox when a slow-moving vehicle meant danger...or death.

Footsteps approached. "You going in or out?"

Tag shook off the tension and forced a smile for

the short lady with a head full of silver-white curls. "Sorry, caught me daydreaming. Please, go ahead." He watched the truck inch around the corner before he stepped over the threshold. *Redmond, get a grip. You're in the good ol' USA, not Afghanistan.* Once inside, he pulled off his sunglasses, tucked them into the neckband of his shirt, and took a deep breath to calm his pulse.

A quick survey of the room provided the layout. A row of teller windows to the left, two private offices to his right, and several desks in an open area. At the far end stood a grouping of chairs with a low table and a clipboard. Must be a sign-in sheet. At the opposite end was an exit door that must lead to an alley or a parking lot. He took a second look to locate the woman with the honey-blonde hair. Third in line for the tellers. Probably, he and the pretty lady would share nothing more than those few seconds at the entrance.

He set off toward the group of chairs, checking to make sure the dogs remained at his side. For the past couple of months, he'd been covering the costs of his dog-training business from his savings. But he wanted to get the kennel runs constructed faster than only one each month. He sat next to the table and waited for Taffy and Pixie to lie at his feet. Then he signed his name on the log and wrote "personal loan." He pulled off his hat and set it on an adjacent chair, nodding when he met the gaze of a seated woman holding a toddler in her lap.

"That man has dogs."

"Yes, Tommy, they're dogs that help people."

"I wanna puppy, Mama."

The woman brushed the boy's dark hair off his forehead. "I know you do."

The bank patrons received his continued surveillance—a situational awareness habit he hadn't yet broken. As he watched the blonde study her phone, he wondered if he could list Brotherhood Protectors as an employer.

Sure, he'd had an interview with Hank and laid out his qualifications. But, technically, he hadn't yet received his first assignment. Hank expressed enthusiasm about Tag's dog handler skills. He even mentioned expanding his security services to include trained guard dogs. In his heart, Tag wondered if he could work on another canine team. So much trust was involved between the working pair. His heart had been just about ripped from his chest when his injury caused Dex to be reassigned to another soldier. Until the kennel was built, he couldn't house big dogs. So, he hadn't been forced to make that decision yet.

The back door banged against the wall with a crash.

"This here's a robbery. Everybody, stay where you are." Three men dressed all in black with balaclavas covering their faces ran to the middle of the room, waving shotguns. "Tellers, hands up. Do not hit the panic buttons if you want to live."

Shit. Straightening, Tag grabbed the chair arms, his pulse kicking up. His instincts about that truck and its occupants had been right.

A woman screamed. Someone cursed.

Both dogs jumped to their feet, bodies stiff. Pixie whimpered.

Tag stilled, his senses firing on high. As he watched the men, he leaned forward, his hand held flat, to signal for the dogs to lie down. The last thing he needed was for them to draw attention or be viewed as threats.

One man ran to the front door and shoved a crow bar through the door handles. With his weapon leveled waist high, a second one stalked the security guard and disarmed him. Then he pulled a can of spray paint from the back of his waistband and sprayed the lenses of the security cameras.

The third grabbed a small, metal trash cash and dumped out the contents. "Put your cell phones in here."

His gaze scanning the men, Tag slid his phone from his right back pocket and slipped it beneath Pixie's training vest, tucked high toward her shoulders. He prayed the unit would stay in place. Lowering himself to the center of the group of chairs, he positioned his body in front of the dogs.

He studied the three men, hoping to spot an identifying gesture or feature. Two looked to be a little under six feet and of average weight.

"Everyone on the ground. Lie yourselves down and don't give us any trouble." The tallest of the group waved his weapon toward those in line and held out the can with the other hand.

"Ma'am," Tag whispered to the shocked woman who sat frozen, clutching her little boy to her chest. "Get behind me." Alternating his gaze between the robbers and her wide-eyed expression, he jerked a thumb over his shoulder, hoping she'd snap out of her terror.

Blinking fast, she nodded, dropped to a crouch, and moved outside of the chair circle, clinging to her fussing child with one hand.

The third robber was a bit over six feet and maybe two hundred pounds. Muscles stretched the sleeves of his black pullover shirt. The robber jabbed an elderly man holding a cane.

Tag cringed, clamping his jaw tight.

"Move it, Gramps. Get on the floor." He stalked close to the silver-haired lady.

The blonde had an arm around the elderly lady's waist and supported the woman's elbow.

"I said lie down." The thief waved the gun in their faces. "Hurry."

"No, please don't." The older woman put up her hands to cover her face and shuddered.

"Just stop." The blonde's head snapped up, and she moved in front of the older woman, blocking her smaller form. "She's doing her best. The lady has a bad hip."

"Sassy, huh?" After dropping the can, he stepped close and grabbed the blonde's arm. "I like a bit of spunk." He leaned close and sniffed. "You sure smell pretty."

Blondie held her ground, chin up, and met his stare.

Silently, Tag cheered her spirit but worried she might push the guy too far. Most bank robbers had a specific timetable to get in, grab the loot, and make their escape. He itched to reach the KA-BAR knife strapped to his left calf. But he was too far away for the blade to have an impact.

"In fact, spunky lady, you're my designated helper."

"I will not." She started to turn back to the other woman.

Quick as a flash, he swung his right arm and back-handed her left cheek.

She cried out and stumbled but didn't go down. Then she tossed her hair over her shoulder and snatched the trash can. After a step to the side, she held it in front of the older woman. "Please do as he says."

Before he realized his movement, Tag rose like he was in PT and doing pushups then placed his strong leg beneath his body. He reached for his knife.

"Hey, got a hero over here." One of the men stepped close and rested the muzzle of the shotgun on Taffy's body. "On your belly, or the dog eats it."

Taffy cowered and looked over her shoulder.

So angry his muscles quivered, Tag lowered his body to the ground. He held an upright hand, palm outward, toward Taffy and Pixie, giving them the signal to stay.

"Gimme your phone." The barrel waved in his direction. "You, too, lady. Slide it over."

She complied, and the robber scooped up the phone.

"Left it in my truck." Tag held his empty hands over his head. Helpless, he watched as the blonde gathered the cell phones, set down the can, and then returned to the older woman's side.

By now, the executives were rousted from their offices and directed to lie on the floor like the others.

One of the robbers moved behind the teller's counter, stuffing money into a black duffle bag. "Number One, I'm not collecting much here. Only small bills. Bring over the president so he can get us into the vault."

"Not the plan, Number Two." The tall one walked backward to the teller's access door, his gun sweeping the room.

The third man yanked on the arm of a middle-aged executive in a suit. "Here he is. I vote with Number Two." He marched the pudgy man the length of the room, where the three robbers argued.

Tag glanced toward the security guard's position, but the man wasn't looking around. *No help from him.* Damn, he cursed the fact he hadn't yet met Montana's residency requirement to get his concealed carry permit. After eight years of having a weapon close by, he felt almost naked without one. Especially now. He looked over at the blonde and met her stare.

A red welt rose on her left cheek. She patted the older woman's wrinkled hand.

Her plaintive gaze called to him. From the twenty-five-foot distance, he couldn't determine the eye color, but the intensity of her gaze created a strong connection. His fingers curled into the synthetic carpet. He wanted to make promises that everything would be all right. But failed or compromised missions had taught him in a hard and gut-busting way to keep his mouth shut in situations he couldn't control. Empty promises were worse than silences.

A siren sounded in the distance, getting closer.

Stupid LEO. Wasn't the local enforcement officer trained to make a silent approach? Tag tensed, knowing this situation could go from bad to worse if the robbers panicked.

"Number One, we gotta split."

Number One ran to the front and glanced outside. "No worries. That's a fire truck. Just turned the corner and is headed in the opposite direction." He looked back toward his gang and gestured his gun in a big circle. "Grab it all."

Number Three shoved the bank president to his knees and moved inside the tellers' area to help. "Wait here."

With all three robbers distracted, Tag rolled to his right side, pulled his knife from its sheath, and held it along his thigh. Inching backward, he angled his body to better view the separated positions of the robbers. He glanced toward the thief near the front, his gaze connecting with the blonde's.

Frowning, she shook her head and mouthed, *no.*

"Mama, look. That man has—"

The rest of the boy's words were muffled.

A horn honked three times in rapid succession from outside.

"Shit." Number One sprinted toward the back of the building. "Number Four's spotted something. Let's haul ass."

Tag slid out his phone from Pixie's vest, punched in his password, and tapped video. Arm slung over Pixie's body, he held the phone near her left shoulder and started recording. He hoped to hell the angle was right to catch footage of these men in action.

Two men burst from the tellers' area, each holding a bag. One of them stooped, grabbed the bank president, and held the surprised man in front of his body. "I've got my human shield." The other robber followed suit.

Before he could blink, Tag saw the blonde hauled to her feet and yanked in front of the tallest robber.

"Let me go." She struggled against his grip and kicked at his shins.

"Stop it, bitch." He cinched an arm around her middle, grabbed a breast, and with the other hand, jammed the gun at her temple. "Now, quit resisting and walk out the damn door."

Turning her head, she cast Tag a wide-eyed look.

Her eyes broadcast a clear plea. At the sight of the guy groping her breast, Tag bit back a protest and clamped his jaw tight. His whole body shook with the effort of not racing to her side. So far, shots hadn't been fired and Tag needed to think of all the hostages.

But someone would pay.

He paced his breathing, readying himself to spring into action once the door started swinging shut. As soon as their backs were turned, he rose to a crouch then eased aside a chair for a clear path.

He launched himself forward, like bursting from the starting blocks of a hundred-yard dash. He ran, wincing at the pull on his wound, and caught the door before it closed.

Not twenty feet from the exit, the two male hostages struggled to push themselves upright from the asphalt. Beyond them, the black truck idled, front door ajar.

"Get inside, bitch." The robber thrashed the blonde from side to side to dislodge her hold and shove her into the front seat.

"Somebody, help me." She fought his actions with a foot braced on the open door and a hand gripped on the doorframe.

"Stay down." Tag pointed at the two men then flipped the knife in his grip, grasped the cool blade, drew back his arm, and threw. Like innumerable times before, he watched the weapon roll end over end. The seven-inch blade hit the intended target— lodging in the robber's upper back.

With an anguished grunt, the robber let go of his captive and stretched a hand behind him, turning in a circle. Not having any luck, he had to grab over his shoulder.

Run, Blondie, run. Tag strode down the shallow incline toward the rear of the parked car to his right.

She lowered her foot to the pavement and angled her body away from the door.

But the driver reached across the seat to grab a handful of blonde hair and pull the screaming and flailing woman inside.

With a glare over his shoulder, the masked man pulled out the knife, leaned inside the cab, and held it against her neck. He slid into the seat next to the subdued hostage and slammed the door as the truck burned rubber out of the parking lot.

Late model, maybe a two-ton pickup. Smeared-on mud covered the vehicle's identifying logos and the license plate. Tag threw back his head and roared, fists clenched at his sides. Not only had he failed to save her, he'd supplied them with a weapon.

CHAPTER 2

HER CELL PHONE CHIMED...AGAIN. Malin Langstrom paced her small studio cabin, knowing what she'd see in the text box. One of her two sisters asking for help with the meal service for the ranch guests. The problem was Malin didn't know if she could walk the hundred yards to Dream Vistas' main house and be in the same room as the registered guests.

Ever since the bank robbery a month ago, she shied away from any and all strangers. Not good for a person who worked in the service industry. The first time someone bumped into her at the grocery store, the mere touch sent her into a panic attack complete with muscle shakes, labored breathing, and narrowed vision. She'd abandoned the half-filled shopping cart and retreated to her car. Only an emergency phone session with her therapist Suzanne calmed her enough to drive home.

Malin stopped at the cabin's front window overlooking a grassy area between buildings. A breeze set the purple wild hyacinth and yellow buttercups waving. The bucolic sight soothed. Normally, she'd be out in the open air, picking wildflowers for table arrangements or weeding the flower beds in front of the cabins and bunkhouse.

Following the trauma, her sisters, Tilda and Jude, were as supportive as they knew how to be. No matter their assurances, Malin recognized she wasn't pulling her weight at the guest ranch they'd inherited upon their parents' deaths five years earlier. She could handle her normal duties of monitoring the ranch's social media presence, booking reservations, and managing the accounts —because none of the tasks involved direct inter-actions with guests. But she used to assist Tilda in the kitchen with meal preparation and pitch in along with Jude to run errands and transport guests to and from local airports.

Malin paced another three lengths of the living space, hands clenched at her sides. *This waffling behavior is ridiculous. I am dependable and efficient, and I can perform simple tasks like set out food.* She sucked in a calming breath. As long as nobody touched her or came too close. She reached to the back of her head and made sure the large clip held her gathered hair in place. After jamming her phone into a back jeans pocket, she walked through the cabin door and turned toward the main house.

Today, the big blue sky held only a few wispy clouds. She trudged through matted prairie grass toward the back deck of the three-story log cabin. Spotting a few guests at the umbrellaed tables set her teeth on edge. A courteous smile was all she could muster before slipping through the sliding glass door, crossing the spacious family room with multiple couches and chairs, and heading down the hallway to the kitchen. "I'm here. What can I do?" The rich smell of frying meat filled the air.

Tilda, older by four years, looked up from the stove and smiled. "Thank you for showing up." She reached to stir a big pot on a back burner. Then she glanced at the island. "Let me think what needs to be done next."

As usual, blonde tendrils escaped the wide barrette at the back of Tilda's neck and hung along her cheeks in wavy strands. An apron printed with "Life is short, lick the bowl" covered the pink T-shirt that matched her own. Long ago, the sisters adopted a color of the day and had shirts screen-printed with the Dream Vistas Ranch logo on the back. The ranch hands wore company T-shirts in gray, green, or wheat.

Malin glanced at the kitchen's center island and spotted the makings for a taco and burrito meal—

always a crowd favorite. She grabbed an apron and slipped the loop over her head. "I didn't notice as I walked through. Are the warming trays set up?"

"Jude was supposed to handle that, but she got called away to sign for a delivery."

"No problem. I'll do it." Malin stepped to the sink and washed her hands then walked to the dining room and crouched in front of the side buffet. In no time, she had the metal stands set up in Tilda's preferred arrangement complete with the cans of warming fuel ready to be lit. Counting out three rectangular metal trays, she stood and carried them into the kitchen.

A tall man blocked the kitchen doorway, his shoulders filling the opening.

Malin skidded to a stop and gulped back her shock. Guests weren't supposed to be in the kitchen during meal preparations. Where had *he* come from?

"Miss." He dipped his chin in greeting then gave her a once-over, his grin widening. "I'm admiring your place here."

"Uh, huh." Biting her lower lip, she glanced around him to where Tilda had been at the stove. Was she alone with him? Her pulse raced, and she scanned the kitchen. Why was this man here? "Excuse me, sir. I need to take these to my sister."

"Sure." With a shrug, he pivoted and walked into the kitchen.

Dots floated across her vision, and she sucked in a fortifying breath. *I will not panic.* The man was a stranger, and she was supposed to enter the room where he was? The trays rattled in her shaking hands. Sucking in a deep breath, she held the metal rectangles in front of her like a shield as she walked through the doorway and moved to the opposite side of the island. "Here are the serving trays."

Jude leaned over the counter, studying a delivery slip. White-blonde hair spiked in all directions from her head. She glanced up and her eyes shot wide. "Hey, Malin. I totally did not know you were here." Facing the man, she gave a beckoning wave. "Gary, come here. Let's go over this delivery together."

"Well, I am." *Focus on the task and shove aside the uncertainty.* Malin moved to the stove, grabbed two potholders, and lifted the huge Dutch oven filled with Spanish rice.

"Here, little lady. Let me carry that." The stranger stepped close with his hands outstretched.

At the brush of his arm against her shoulder, she froze. Memories of being manhandled played though her mind. "Don't!" Her voice was sharper than she intended. Without looking up, she muttered an apology. "Only ranch employees can handle food, per our license." In her peripheral vision, she saw Jude and Tilda exchange an arched-eyebrow look. *Focus.*

"Gary, I checked the delivery slip against my order." Jude waved the paper in the air. "Let's go unload the supplies."

Gary headed in her direction. "I'll unload, and you can check off the items."

Jude matched his strides toward the front door. "Now, are you implying women can't do the physical work?"

Malin breathed out a sigh of relief at their fading voices. She leaned a hip against the island and relaxed her body.

"You all right?"

The concern in her sister's voice brought tears to Malin's eyes, and she blinked them away. When would these irrational fears end? Malin nodded then scooped steaming rice from the pot into the tray. From years of practice, the women gathered all the condiments needed for the meal. Soon, the buffet's surface was filled with fresh guacamole, sour cream, grated cheese, jalapeno peppers, and three types of salsa.

"I'll announce the meal is ready." Tilda moved toward the back deck to where the meal bell hung on the wall. "Will you bring in the pitchers of iced tea?"

"I will." Ringing sounded at the same time a vibration buzzed her butt cheek. Malin didn't recognize the number, but seeing the Montana area code, she swiped the pulsing bar. "Hello?"

"Miss Malin Langstrom?"

The voice was firm, deep, but unfamiliar. Her pulse quickened. "Speaking."

"Detective James Rayburn here, calling from the Butte-Silver Bow Sheriff's Department."

Detective. Her grip tightened. "Go ahead."

"Multiple suspects in last month's bank robbery have been arrested. We'd like you to come in and view a line-up to see if you recognize anyone."

She'd been hoping for, and yet dreading, a call like this one. Shoulders slumping, she leaned a hip against the counter. "Did you read the report I provided? I never saw any of their faces."

"Miss Langstrom, we understand the crew wore masks. But you did hear their voices." A chair creaked. "You were the closest to the men for the longest amount of time."

A chill ran down her spine. She didn't need to be reminded how the robbers drove around for ten minutes, evading responding law enforcement vehicles, before dumping her in the parking lot of an abandoned warehouse. Her throat tightened. "When?" She lifted her head to look across the room toward the rooster-shaped clock on the wall. Twelve forty-five.

"This afternoon would be best, either two-thirty or three o'clock. Or tomorrow morning."

She needed to change clothes plus allow for the drive time. God, she did not want to fulfill this duty. "I'm an hour away and can't be there until three."

"See you then. Corner of North Alaska and Quartz in Butte."

With a shaky finger, she punched the red button to end the call.

"Malin, where is the iced tea?" Tilda scurried into the room then her eyes rounded. "What's happened? You look so pale."

"Sheriff wants me to view a line-up." Malin moved to the commercial refrigerator and pulled out four plastic pitchers of tea.

"Oh, sweetie, when?" Tilda gripped the edge of the island. "I'll come with you."

"You can't afford the time. I'll be fine by myself." *I have to be.* Grabbing two handles in each hand, she lifted the pitchers and walked to the dining room. Now, because many of the guests were already seated, she'd have to make a circuit of the occupied tables. Although her stomach roiled so much she thought she'd puke, Malin poured servings of tea and smiled like a gracious hostess for the next ten minutes. She *would* get past this experience and recover to where serving the guests again came naturally.

Almost two hours later, Malin pulled into the public parking lot at the dead-end stub of Quartz Street. She hurried across the two-lane street toward the imposing three-story Justice Center at the intersection. Gray stones—some smooth and some rough—created the blocky first floor. Beige bricks formed the upper two floors, complete with a corniced overhanging roofline and roaring gargoyles guarding the building corners.

For the past ten minutes, she'd recited affirmations aloud to bolster her courage. Now, she had to act on that trumped-up confidence. Once inside, she followed directions to the detective's office, walking along the outside of a grouping of desks, and knocked on the wooden jamb of the opened door. "Detective Rayburn?"

"Yes." A burly-chested man with thinning black hair and bushy eyebrows looked up from paperwork spread on his desk. "Miss Langstrom?"

Swallowing hard, she nodded.

"Come inside." The detective, dressed in a blue shirt and gray slacks, stood and swept a hand toward two wooden chairs against the wall. "Have a seat." He moved around the desk.

Gasping at his approach, she scooted sideways and grabbed the top of a chair to steady herself.

He stopped, his brows wrinkling. "I'm headed to close the door for privacy. Is that all right?"

Malin scurried to the chair farthest from the door. "That's fine." She tucked her purse at her feet and clasped her hands in her lap.

The big man closed the door and stepped to the front of his desk, sitting on the edge. "The process you'll go through is straightforward. I'll take you to a room that overlooks another room where several men will be positioned directly under a number. You'll watch through a one-way window, and they can't see you. Normally, a witness is asked to view the assembled line-up for a visual identification. But since the crew wore masks, we'll have them read a script compiled from witness statements. Hopefully, you'll recognize a voice."

"Okay." Her mouth dried. The robbery replayed often enough in her mind she'd never forget the one thief who'd slapped and groped her. If only the voice was all she remembered. Dread weighted her muscles. "I'll try."

"Remember, Miss Langstrom, the men will neither hear nor see you. You'll be safe."

The reassuring note in his voice indicated she must look more scared than she thought. "I appreciate that. I'm ready." Her hands trembled as she reached for her purse and stood. The faster she completed this process, the sooner she could return to the safety of the ranch…and her sisters. Malin followed through a maze of short corridors between offices, a room with a copier and shelves holding supplies, and an area with vending machines. The sound of ringing phones faded the farther she walked.

Detective Rayburn stopped at a door marked "Observation" and twisted the knob.

Pressing a hand against her jumpy stomach, she turned sideways then stepped inside and positioned herself in front of the glass. The room was painted a pale green except for the numerals one through six on the opposing wall a foot below the ceiling. Corresponding numerals designated selected spots on the concrete floor.

The detective stepped to a metal speaker on the wall next to the window and pushed a button. "Officer Daley, walk in the line-up."

Hugging her purse to her chest, she steeled herself for what was to come. The door opened, and six men of varying heights and shapes entered.

"Move along and stand on a number. Hands at your side." The officer, wearing a navy-blue uniform, leaned against the door with feet braced apart. His hands rested on his bulky belt.

She scanned the men, noting hair colors from dark to light and styles from buzz cut to shaggy. When viewed together, the men exhibited relatively similar heights—none very short or very tall. All sported average builds. Their facial features meant nothing. She shook her head. "I'm sorry."

"That's all right." Detective Rayburn punched the button. "Pass the first one the card, Daley."

The uniformed officer pulled a white card from his back pocket and passed it to the average-sized man with dark hair in the number-one position. "Read this and speak up."

The man glanced at the card then looked at the officer. "The whole thing?"

Daley nodded.

"This here's a robbery. Everybody stay where you are."

Goose flesh rose on Malin's skin. The words from that day hit hard, the shock kicking up her pulse.

"Tellers, hands up. Do not hit the panic buttons if you want to live. Put your cell phones in this can. Everyone on the ground. Lie down and don't give us any trouble. Move it, Gramps. Get on the floor. Sassy, huh? I like a bit of spunk."

During the robbery, the last two sentences had been spoken just to her. Hearing them again chilled her blood. She closed her eyes, and the incident flashed through her mind in slow motion. Hazel eyes under brown eyebrows surrounded by the cloth mask. A crooked front incisor and a scar under his nose. Had she remembered those details the first time? Her eyes shot open as the man continued reading, and she studied their faces, but the distance was too great to see a scar. She gulped in a breath of stuffy air, hearing a faint buzzing in her ears.

"You sure smell pretty. In fact, spunky lady, you're my designated helper. Hey, got a hero over here. On your belly, or the dog eats it. Gimme your phone. You, too, lady. Slide it over. Number One, I'm not collecting much here. Only small bills. Bring over the president so he can get into the vault. Not the plan, Number Two. Here he is. I vote with Number Two. Number One, we gotta split. No worries. That's a fire truck. Just turned the corner and is headed in the opposite direction. Grab it all. Wait here. Shit. Number Four's spotted something. Let's haul ass. I've got my human shield."

Her stomach knotted. She braced herself for the next part, her skin crawling at the memory of the man's rough touch on her body. How he'd groped her breast to gain her compliance.

"Stop it, bitch. Now, walk out that door. Get inside, bitch."

The tone wasn't right—too nasal. She opened her eyes and glanced at the detective. "Not him. Could I please have a chair?"

"Of course." He opened the door and stepped outside. Within seconds, he returned with a molded plastic one and set it in the middle of the window.

By the time she'd listened to the audio version of the robbery five more times, Malin was a shivering wreck. She finished the bottle of water the detective brought, but her tongue felt as dry as a slab of jerky. Perspiration wet her blouse's collar, and her bra chafed with dampness.

A throat cleared. "Miss Langstrom, are you ready to sign your statement?"

She glanced up and gazed at the surroundings, surprised at the bookshelf and desk. They'd moved from the observation room to the detective's office.

He slid a document forward on a cleared spot on his desk.

Malin lifted the paper and scanned the printed text. She'd recognized two of the voices—numbers three and six. During both of the men's readings of the script, she'd experienced a roiling of her stomach and a breakout of nervous sweat. "I agree with what's printed here. Where do I sign?" This statement might get two members of the crew off the street. But what about the others?

Moments later, she stood on the sidewalk in front of the sheriff's department and breathed fresh air. Now, she wished she'd let Tilda come along. Her vision kept narrowing and zooming out, making her dizzy. Traffic moved but the sounds were muted. In this nervous state, she doubted her ability to safely drive home. Nothing seemed real— like she wasn't actually in touch with the physical surroundings. She leaned a hand on the gray stone, still cool on this spring day. The structure was solid and would keep her grounded in reality.

Walking close to the building, she rounded the corner on shaky legs and inched a halting path toward the parking lot. Toward the end of the street, a couple of women talking with their heads close together walked in her direction. Behind her, vehicles drove along Alaska Street, but the sounds remained distant, meaning no one turned onto this dead-end street. She stopped only a couple times to catch her breath, hoping her heart rate would return to normal. Did she need to call Suzanne? Or could she work though this panic attack on her own? If she followed her normal coping routine, then the panic should subside...like on the other occasions.

The beige ranch truck with the Dream Vistas logo on the driver's door stood within sight. But the span across the two lanes of asphalt and five slots deep into the lot stretched impossibly far. Almost as if each step she took moved the goal an equal distance away.

Fumbling inside her purse, she wrapped her fingers around her cell phone and dragged out her earbuds. Plugged in, she scrolled for her empowerment playlist and let "Fight Song" roll through her mind. Strengthened, she absorbed Cher's voice singing "Woman's World" and those lyrics carried her across the street. "You Haven't Seen the Last of Me" got her to the truck, and she jumped inside. The cocoon of the truck's cab surrounded and protected her. She slumped back against the seat, escaping into the rhythm of the pounding drumbeats. By the time the lyrics of "I Am Woman" sounded, Malin sang along, bopping her head, with tears of release streaming down her cheeks.

A rap-rap against the window wrenched a scream from her throat. She froze then eased her head to the side.

Outside stood a tall, muscled man hunched over to eye level, his face shaded under a straw cowboy hat.

"Go away! I don't have any cash." Scrunching her eyes closed, she shook her head and slapped a hand on the armrest until she heard the door locks click. What should she do? Her pulse spiked, shattering the calm she'd achieved. She grabbed for her key ring and inserted the correct one into the ignition.

"I'm not looking for money, miss."

Panting shallow breaths, Malin glanced sideways to see the man had backed away and stood with palms raised. *I have to get away.* She cranked over the engine and reached for the gear shift lever. Then she heard a dog yip. Turning, she spied a tricolored dog with floppy ears wearing a red vest being held at window height. The horrible day of the robbery replayed in her mind. She remembered the tall cowboy who'd held open the bank's door accompanied by dogs wearing the same vest. She punched the window lever until the pane lowered a couple inches. Then she gazed into the same brown eyes where she'd looked for reassurance during those awful twenty minutes.

"Hi. Remember me?" The handsome man smiled, displaying a shallow dimple in his left cheek.

For the first time since that traumatic day, she spread her lips in a natural smile. How could she forget her hero?

CHAPTER 3

HER SUNNY SMILE kicked up Tag's heart rate. If only her response was meant for him. Most likely, she reacted to Pixie's head tilt and panting tongue visible through the truck window. "Sorry if I scared you." Her eyes were the prettiest blue he'd ever seen, and he could keep gazing into them for hours. Too soon her smile faded, and he didn't like how she wouldn't maintain eye contact. The urge to reassure her rose. He rested a hand on the passenger door.

She glanced down, her gaze narrowing as she chewed her lower lip. Then she looked up again. "I've been a bit jumpy since…"

"Yeah, I'll bet." Ever since the black truck sped out of sight that dark day, he'd been worried about that type of reaction. While giving his statement at the scene, he'd heard the officer's radio announce the hostage had been located. The intense relief he'd felt then mirrored what he felt at finally meeting her. An officer must have driven her to the sheriff's department because he hadn't seen her again that day. "I met with the detective probably for the same reason you did. I wanted to introduce myself. Tag Redmond." He shifted Pixie, tucking the dog under his left arm then extended his hand.

Frowning, she cringed away from the window before gripping the steering wheel with both hands. "I'm Malin Langstrom. But I really need to be getting back to...um, home."

No shit, she's jumpy. "Sure. I just thought..." What had he thought? That he'd get her number and call for a date? "I wanted to make sure you're doing all right."

"I will be fine." After powering up the window, she adjusted the gearshift. The truck rolled backward.

He stepped to the front of the parking slot. The determined note in her voice didn't match the haunted look in her eyes or the shaking of her hands. At least, they'd finally met, and he learned her name. As he watched the truck exit the lot and turn left, he noticed the ranch logo and read the business name painted on the door, making a mental note.

Pixie wiggled and licked his hand.

Tag crouched to set Pixie's feet on the ground.

Then he stood, told the dog to heel, and strode toward his truck at the far end of the parking spaces.

From nearby, an engine roared to life and revved.

Sudden noises still caught his attention and put him on high alert. He scanned the immediate area and saw no occupants in the parked vehicles. Then he glanced over his shoulder and froze, his pulse kicking up.

A black king-cab truck rolled along the path Malin had taken.

Shit. His skin prickled. That same truck was at the robbery. "Let's run, Pixie." He jogged toward the back of the lot, pulling his cell phone from his pocket. After reaching the vehicle, he yanked on the door handle and lifted Pixie into the backseat, clipping on her travel harness. Then he scrolled through his contacts and punched the one for Rayburn as he hopped behind the wheel. "Detective, Tag Redmond. Spotted suspect's truck." He hit the button for Speaker and set the phone in a cup holder before putting the vehicle in motion.

"Where?"

"Outside your office. In pursuit now." He turned right onto North Alaska and scanned the vehicles ahead. Her beige truck already waited at the next intersection. "No license visible."

"Give me your exact location."

"Alaska and Granite." Waiting for the light to change, he drummed his fingers on the wheel.

"Geez, you are close."

"Driver probably waited for either of us but followed her exit." He turned right then checked his mirrors and signaled to maneuver into Malin's lane. In the background, he heard Rayburn yelling instructions to the dispatcher. "Crap."

"What?"

"Dumbass driver wouldn't let me change lanes." After several seconds passed, he eased the truck left and waved a hand to the trailing car. "I'm assuming she's headed to one of the southbound streets that connect with the interstate."

"Probably Montana."

Tag glanced at the street sign. "Correct. Left there. Which onramp will she use—north or south?" At the sign of the yellow light, he punched the accelerator and tapped the horn before racing through the intersection. He hated to draw attention, but he couldn't let the vehicles get too far ahead.

Pixie whimpered as her nails scratched against the seat.

"Can't tell you that."

"Damn it, Rayburn." He pounded a fist on the wheel. "Have you got the resources to protect her?" He pulled into the same lane as the black truck, keeping a compact car between their vehicles.

Squinting, he searched for a reflection in the truck's side mirror. But the window tint was too dark to see the occupants. "Does she even live in your county?"

"I'll contact Sheriff Bar—uh, the sheriff where she's headed and let him know what's going on. That's the best I can do."

Had he been about to say Barron? The sheriff of the Eagle Rock department. Tag pulled a fisted hand downward, elbow tucked at his side. Something finally went right. "I'm driving a 2009 red four-by-four with Wyoming plates. Tell the responding officers I'm the good guy." He ended the call then picked up the phone. Glancing between his driving and the screen, he scrolled through his contacts until he found Hank Patterson and hit Call. He really had to get a hands-free headset.

"Brotherhood Protectors. Hank here."

"Hank, Tag Redmond."

"Hey, Tag. How are—"

"Listen up. I'm tailing a vehicle I suspect is connected to last month's Butte bank robbery."

A chair creaked, and tapping sounded on a keyboard. "Got a license number? I'll check my resources."

"Plate's missing." He drove through another intersection, keeping his gaze on the light-colored top of Malin's truck. "Do you know Dream Vistas Ranch?"

"Yeah, I do. A guest ranch north of town owned by the Langstrom sisters."

Bingo. "One of them was a witness, too, and the suspect truck is following her." Tag wondered if she spotted the tail and how she reacted.

"Damn. Then they're headed this way. How far back are you?"

"Two car lengths. Soon as I hit the interstate, I'm sliding between the vehicles." The scumbag won't run her off the road. Not on his watch. *Huh.* "I might have created my first assignment."

"Got no agents free right now to send your way. Drive here as soon as you can. Stay safe."

"Roger. Redmond out." He tapped the screen, drove under the freeway overpass, and accelerated onto the two-lane divided I90/15 highway. The traffic was heavier than when he'd driven north, but it wasn't too bad. Additional vehicles provided good cover. Within three miles, he positioned himself in the fast lane a car length behind the black truck.

Malin stuck to the posted speed limit.

Tag checked the rearview mirror and spotted a sheriff's SUV hanging back about one hundred yards. The more he thought about the situation, the more convinced he became the deputy probably couldn't pull over the suspect's vehicle unless the driver made a stupid blunder.

Tag crept forward and then signaled to ease the truck into the slow lane. Once there, he allowed a safe distance between their trucks then set the cruise control. Short of hauling Malin into his own vehicle, he'd done what he could to protect her. His grip on the wheel loosened, and he flexed his fingers. Rolling his shoulders, he glanced around. Clouds stacked up along the ridge of the Crazy Mountains to the west. *Might get a little rain later.*

The next time he looked in his rearview mirror, he spotted a yellow SUV behind him and glanced over his shoulder to verify the black truck was gone. Moving sideways in his lane revealed the trailing car was a blue sedan. Tensing, he glanced in all directions. Where was the law enforcement vehicle? Then he remembered seeing a sign for Madison County. Out of Butte-Silver Bow's jurisdiction.

Time for a new plan. He steered into the left lane until he drew abreast of Malin's truck then honked. Her head didn't turn. He eased forward a few feet and honked again, adding a big wave.

Malin glanced over, and her eyes widened.

He pointed to his chest and then toward the upcoming ramp exit sign. Seeing her nod, he pulled ahead and flipped on his right turn signal. Tag held his breath as two then three seconds passed before he spotted her signal flash. Past the next city street, he pulled over onto the shoulder then jogged back to her vehicle.

"Why are you following me?" Malin frowned over the partially lowered window.

"Did you see the black truck on your tail since you left the sheriff's department?"

"Holy crap." Gasping, she shook her head and glanced over her shoulder. "Was it the one from the robbery?"

Tag rested a hand on the window frame so he could bend over, the heat registered on his fingers. "I think so. I want to take you to meet a friend who can help with this situation."

"I met you for the first-time minutes ago. Why would I go with you anywhere?" Head shaking, she powered up the window. "I should never have left the ranch."

"No, wait." He took a deep breath. He'd seen her panic in the parking lot near the sheriff's department. So, he had to act calm and rational. A lot rested on how he phrased his next statement. "Have you heard of Hank Patterson and Brotherhood Protectors?"

The window dropped three inches. An eyebrow arched, and she tilted her head. "I have. Last fall, one of Hank's agents helped my cousin, Caitlyn."

"Will you follow me to his ranch so the three of us can discuss a way to protect you?"

Mouth pressed tight, she gripped the wheel and stared straight ahead.

That he couldn't see her eyes or know what she might be feeling bothered him. More than he could have predicted. Tag watched her lips move but couldn't hear what she said.

"What's the name of Hank's ranch?"

Smart girl to verify what I know. "White Oak Ranch."

"And the name of his child."

On his first visit to the Brotherhood Protectors headquarters, he'd met Hank's beautiful wife, Sadie, and saw her with a chubby-cheeked girl. But he hadn't paid much attention. He ran a hand through his close-cropped hair. "Um, blonde hair and blue eyes. Emma? No, her name's Emily."

She shot him a glance and then looked forward again.

"Malin, I'm an ex-Army Ranger with eight years of service. My goal is to find a way to make you feel secure." For a strange reason, he wanted her agreement more than he'd wanted anything in recent months. "Trust me, please."

"All right, I'll follow you."

"Great." He turned toward his truck and almost missed hearing her final whispered words.

"I trust you."

Those soft words, spoken so hesitantly, confirmed the need to protect her. A lump formed in his throat. *I will not let you down this time, Malin Langstrom.*

WHY DID I AGREE? Malin kept her gaze on the tailgate of the red truck ahead. True, the dark-haired man knew the basics about the Patterson family. But did that fact alone mean he was trustworthy? He had dark brown eyes that looked as deep as a vat of chocolate. Plus dogs were a valid indicator of a solid character. She doubted they'd be calm around someone who wasn't good at heart.

She blew out a harsh breath and tightened her grip. Just because the man's persona made her heart flutter faster than normal didn't mean she should rely on the guy. In agitation, she tapped a thumb on the wheel. So much had been affecting her habits this past month, she wondered if she could count on her own judgment. Maybe she needed to hear the voice of reason.

Ahead, the right turn signal of Tag's truck lit and blinked. The upcoming off ramp exited the freeway several miles north of Eagle Rock. One exit before the one that led to Dream Vistas. After slowing for the westward turn, she drove along fenced pastures where horses and cattle grazed. When the road started to climb into the foothills, she grabbed her phone headset then punched in a preset number. "Suzanne, are you free?"

"Malin, hello. I have about five minutes. How can I help you?"

"I sat through a lineup of robbery suspects today, and I had another attack." The memory of its intensity still shook her nerves. She slowed for a hairpin curve, hoping her cell reception held through the thickly wooded area she'd just entered. "Why aren't the attacks going away? Shouldn't I be farther along in my recovery?" She hated the wimpy whine in her voice, but Malin wanted to return to the confident person she'd been before the robbery.

"Possibly, the time's right for you to step outside of the safe world you've constructed. Stretch your comfort zone and do something for others. A few weeks ago, I met the director of the Brighter Days Rehab Ranch, which I believe is located not far from where you live. Her name's Hannah Davila. Read up on the therapeutic advantages of working with animals. You might want to check out the place."

The name sounded familiar. Malin probably heard something about it from one of her sisters. She loved animals and rode her mare, Stormy, at least twice a week.

Brake lights ahead flashed as the red truck rolled into a clearing and pulled to a stop.

"Gotta go. I'll think about your suggestion. Thanks." She parked a few feet away from Tag's truck and looked up at a large, two-story cabin with huge windows. The setting was almost as beautiful as where she lived. The Crazy Mountains rose on one side and a view of the valley spread in the other. Climbing from the car, she heard the babble of a nearby creek. With eyes closed, she took a deep breath of tangy evergreens, earthy vegetation, and the sweetness of early blooming wildflowers. For the first time in several hours, the tension from the experience at the sheriff's office released. Her body relaxed.

"Peaceful, isn't it?"

At the deep voice, Malin jumped then turned and offered a smile. "I agree." She looked at the tall man who stood a few feet away. Every detail about him screamed capable and confident male. A brown T-shirt fit tight enough to highlight honed shoulders and carved chest. Camouflage-colored cargo pants hugged lean hips. Somehow, the straw Stetson and tooled leather boots completed the picture of this soldier-cowboy.

"Ready to go inside? I know Hank's waiting."

Shaking away her errant thoughts, she nodded and grabbed her purse. "If you think this discussion is necessary." The farther she'd driven from Butte, the less she believed the possibility the robbery suspects had been inside the truck Tag spotted.

How would they have known she'd be at the justice center at any given time? In Montana, trucks probably outnumbered other vehicles two to one, and black was not an unusual color.

"I do." He collected the dog from the back seat and let her run to the end of her leash to relieve herself. "Pixie, heel."

Malin couldn't help smiling at how the little dog always glanced upward for the next command. Poor thing had a long way to look. Walking beside Tag, Malin felt dwarfed, even with her five-foot-seven height. The weight of his hand pressed to her lower back caused a shiver to run through her insides. But she didn't pull away—the first unsolicited touch that hadn't created a knot in her stomach.

The screen door swung outward. "Come on in." Hank waved them inside. "Hello, Malin." He extended his hand. "Tag."

"Thanks for seeing us." Nodding an acknowledgement, she glanced at the ex-Navy SEAL who kept himself in good physical shape. A man in his early thirties, he probably still turned heads with those deep green eyes. She followed him into an office that overlooked the broad valley and sat in front of his desk.

Hank rested his forearms on the desktop in the space between a computer monitor and an inbox stacked with files. "I was sorry to learn you were a victim of the crew responsible for the bank robbery."

She tensed, her grip tightening on the chair arm. Every time she heard that word 'victim' she rebelled. She hated that label. "Just in the wrong place at the wrong time. At least, that's what I keep telling myself."

"Good." Hank gave her a smile. "Positive thinking helps."

Tag maneuvered the dog to sit between their chairs then laid the leash over his thigh. "Well, all the positive thinking in the world won't change the fact I spotted a tail on Malin today. That same truck was still missing a back-license plate with the identifying logos removed."

"I was hoping we'd get more to go on." Hank scrubbed a hand down his face. "A lot of trucks drive on Montana roads."

Exactly my thought. She and Tag were perfect examples of his statement. A weight, followed by warmth, pressed against her ankle. Malin glanced down to see the dog curled up next to her foot. The gesture was kind of sweet. Since the family pet, Skipper, walked the rainbow bridge a few years back, the only dogs on Dream Vistas were owned by a couple of the ranch hands and lived in the barn. Maybe she should make a point of getting down there more often.

Tag scooted forward, his elbows resting on his

knees. "Rayburn said he'd call Barron and give him an update. Do you have enough pull with the local sheriff to gather any intel?"

"Not really." Hank flattened his mouth. "Sorry, but Joe shares only when a threat is imminent. On occasion, he's verified facts when I supply specific identifying data."

Malin shot sideways glances toward the intense man on her left. His rigid posture and stiff expression shouted his displeasure at the news. "I'm sure I'll be fine. My everyday activities don't take me to Butte very often."

"Are you still using the security system Morgan installed at your ranch last fall?"

"Rhys did that?" She slumped back in her chair. Tilda hired him as a ranch hand, but he'd really been acting as an undercover Brotherhood Protector to guard her cousin, Caitlyn. "Before he came, we used a service with devices that monitored the doors and windows and relayed information to an offsite company." Guilt stabbed her as she realized how lax they'd been. "Unfortunately, guests were always setting it off, because they snuck outside to the hot tub or for late-night stargazing." As she spoke, she noticed the wide-eyed expressions on both men's faces. "We got dinged for each incidence after the third false alarm, and thinking of the budget, I cancelled the service."

"You cancelled it?" Tag's dark brows crashed downward.

At the raised voice, the dog perked up and stared at her owner.

Malin leaned away. What gave Tag the right to yell?

"So, you have no way of knowing if unauthorized personnel encroach on the perimeter late at night?" He pushed to his feet and paced to the window.

"Tag." Hank frowned and shook his head then angled his body to face front. "Malin, what Tag should have said is that we need to analyze the ranch's layout and check for ingress points."

Her head swam with the unfamiliar terms. "I'm sorry, but I don't understand what you're asking. Dream Vistas is a customer service operation with a variety of people coming and going throughout each day. Not to mention the service and delivery companies. Guests are booked solid from now until the snow is deep enough to block the roads."

Glancing toward the computer screen, Hank punched at the keyboard. "Can you get your hands on the original blueprints from when the place was built? Or from the last time improvements were made?"

Blueprints? Too complicated. She scooted forward and rested a hand on Hank's desk. "Probably. But I don't see how all this effort is necessary. Two of the thieves are in custody. Although I don't know exactly what role the two played in the robbery, I'm sure the sheriff in Butte has leads on tracking down the other two." With a slow move, she slipped her foot from under the dog, reluctant to disturb its little nap. "I'll call my cousin in St. Paul and ask about the equipment you say Rhys used. Maybe he left it behind. He'll tell us what we need to do to reconnect it, and then the ranch will be secure." She stood. "Really, you two don't need to concern yourselves."

Tag whirled and stalked across the room. "Don't brush us off, Malin. I am concerned. The people in that black truck saw your vehicle the same as I did today in Butte. You drove there in a company truck that advertised the ranch. Now they know you're associated in some way with Dream Vistas."

Gasping, she could only stare. For stability, she leaned a hip against the desk. She'd been driving ranch vehicles for so long she never gave a thought to what was painted on the side doors. Her stomach knotted and roiled. Had cooperating with the investigation put those she loved in danger?

CHAPTER 4

THE NEXT MORNING, after the breakfast rush was over, Malin sat in the dining room, lingering over a cup of coffee with Tilda and Jude. So far, she couldn't bring herself to reveal yesterday's events. Operating the ranch put a big enough burden on them all, and she didn't want to add anything more. But remaining silent wasn't an option, either. "Remember Caitlyn's visit last fall?"

Jude straightened. "Well, that topic is out of the blue. Of course, we remember seeing our favorite cousin."

Nodding, Tilda sipped, but her gaze over the rim of the mug was steady.

Malin ran a finger along the outside of the ceramic handle. "Did she ever mention anything about Rhys placing surveillance equipment around the big house?"

"Not specifically." Tilda set down her mug. "But I gave Rhys permission and access because he was hired to protect her. Why are you asking?"

The next bit would be the hard part. "You know I had an appointment with a detective in Butte yesterday, right?" She paused until she spotted nods from both women. "I went there to identify suspects, but only two of the four have been arrested. Two others are still roaming free." A sigh blew between her lips.

"What does that mean?" Tilda stretched out a hand across the table.

Malin accepted her big sister's finger squeeze. "They saw the ranch truck. Tag seems to think they might show up at the ranch."

"From Butte to here and they're laying low? Hardly." Jude pulled up a crooked leg, spread out her crinkled skirt, and rested her chin on her knee. "Wait, who's Tag?"

Jude would fixate on that one detail in Malin's revelation. Ever since she started seeing her artist friend, Gabriel, she'd looked at every association as a potential relationship. "Another witness from the robbery."

"The one with the dark brown eyes who helped calm you without a single word?" She bobbed her head, and her white-blonde spiky hairdo hardly moved.

"He was helpful that day, and I ran into him

again outside the sheriff's department." She shredded pieces from the edge of the paper napkin and twisted them.

"And...?" Tilda frowned toward Malin's hands. "Whatever happened bothered you, so spill it."

"He thinks I was followed partway home and that we need surveillance here at the ranch." There, she'd shared the facts as she knew them. What she didn't share was how safe she felt when Tag was nearby and how she wished he'd get hired on like Rhys had. Not that she and her sisters could afford to hire a bodyguard. An idea that was just-plain silly because he had his own life. "I texted Caitlyn early this morning and asked her to have Rhys contact me. On the off-chance he left equipment here, I figured he could explain how to reconnect it."

"I wish the expense hadn't forced us to cancel the previous service." Tilda twirled her empty mug on the table. "I would feel much better knowing we had some type of security in place. Especially with your news about being followed."

"But the black truck never reached Eagle Rock. Tag said they disappeared around the Madison county line."

"Hmm." Jude grinned and waggled her eyebrows. "How much time did you spend with him?"

Malin shrugged, hoping to look more nonchalant than she felt. "He accompanied me to discuss the situation with Hank Patterson."

"Hank?" Flopping back in her chair, Tilda sucked in a breath. "So, the issue is that serious."

Guilt flamed her cheeks, and Malin couldn't meet her sisters' gazes. "I'm sorry. I knew nothing good would come out of attending that lineup."

"Don't say that." Jude scooted her chair close and slung an arm over Malin's shoulders. "If you can put these robbers behind bars, more power to you."

Ready to move on to a new topic, Malin stood. "Hank needs a copy of the latest blueprints or architect drawings for the property. Will I find those in Daddy's study?" Even five years following his passing, she couldn't think of the room in any other way.

Jude hopped up. "I know right where they are." She walked from the room with long strides.

"How are you doing, really?" Tilda stood and gathered the mugs and spoons.

Her sister's concerned tone tightened her throat. Malin hated having to admit to her weakness. "Had another attack, but I worked through it on my own." She brushed into a pile the shredded twists she'd made. "I'm considering driving over to Brighter Days this afternoon. Suzanne recommended the place as a way for me to look outward."

"The rehab ranch?" Tilda smiled and nodded. "I think it's a great idea."

In the lull between lunch and dinner preparation, Malin slipped into the decade-old compact she'd owned since her college days. Thankfully, one of the ranch hands, Ryan, liked tinkering with engines as well as tending horses. He kept all the ranch vehicles in top shape.

She set her phone on the passenger seat, the screen displaying an open map application. After sliding on sunglasses, she drove off the Dream Vistas property and turned toward Eagle Rock. Every minute or so, she check her mirrors for a sighting of a black truck. The conversation with Hank and Tag spooked her enough to be more vigilant about her surroundings. Within a few minutes, her shoulders ached from the tension.

Following the computer-voiced directions, ten minutes later she steered onto the road leading to the rehab ranch. As she crept along the drive, she gazed among fenced pastures with grazing horses, a big red barn, a weathered bunkhouse set a hundred feet or so behind, and a rambling, two-story ranch house.

Movement at the side of the barn caught her eye, and she braked to a stop. She figured her trip today would be just to look over the facilities. Baby steps to her recovery. From reading the ranch's website, she learned rehabilitative services were provided to both wounded ex-soldiers and rescue animals. Malin spotted that same philosophy being put into action. Through the windshield, she watched two men lugging a deep, metal pan toward a metal trough. Amputees who'd each lost an arm, they positioned the load so it balanced between their remaining ones. *Clever.*

After shoving her phone into her pocket, she grabbed the car keys and headed toward the barn. At the threshold, she paused, uncertain of who she might find within. Barns were huge structures, and she shouldn't feel trapped like she had yesterday in the ranch kitchen. Once inside, she stopped and waited for her vision to adjust to the darkened interior. Dust motes danced in the sunlight beaming through an overhead window. Earthy scents of cut hay and animal sweat teased her nose. All as familiar as an old robe wrapping her in comfort.

"Let me grab those leads and be right back, Hannah." Someone stepped through the open double doors then skidded. "Oh, can I help you?"

Turning, Malin spotted an older man with gray sprinkled through his brown hair. "Hi, I'm looking for the ranch manager, Hannah. Is she outside?"

"Yes, ma'am. I'm the foreman, Percy Pearson." He removed his gloves and slapped them against his thigh. "Who might you be?"

As long as he remained where he was, his presence didn't upset her. Of course, that fact could be because of the deep laugh lines near his eyes. "Malin. I read about the ranch online and wanted to see it for myself."

"Percy, whose car is that?" A blonde woman came in from outside and glanced between the two already there.

Malin gave a wave. "That's mine." She extended her hand and took a step closer. "I'm Malin Langstrom, one of the three sisters who own and run Dream Vistas Ranch. I was curious about the operation here and wondered if you accepted volunteers."

Hannah rubbed her palm on the back of her jeans and shook hands. "Hannah Ken, um, Davila." She grinned and shook her head. "I haven't been married long and am still getting used to my new last name."

"Ah, congratulations. I read about your wedding in the newspaper." Malin bit back a sigh. At one time, marriage had been a goal toward the top of her life achievement list. Since the robbery experience, she acknowledged the need to get over her panic attacks before she could even entertain the idea of dating.

"Volunteer, huh? We always have more chores than working hands to finish them." She waved toward the back of the barn. "Will you walk with me while I finish a task I'd just started? I can give you a rundown of our operation as we walk."

"Sure." Malin stepped beside the shorter woman who moved with purpose deeper into the barn. She listened to a description of the services that, although Hannah must have given the talk dozens of times, was spoken with enthusiasm. Instantly, she liked this lively person who obviously cared about helping both people and animals. They went through a back door into a small pasture that held a few multi-colored goats.

"Oh, look at the cute goats. I had a childhood friend back in Minnesota whose family raised them." She watched as the yearlings gathered close to a very pregnant doe.

"I need to give Lolita here a quick deworming injection. Don't I, little lady? You'll let me do this without having to chase you." As she talked, Hannah walked with slow steps until she hooked a lead onto the nanny goat's halter. "Since you've been around goats before, Malin, can you hold her lead while I focus on administering the shot?"

"I can handle that." Malin walked forward, holding out her left hand with fingers pointing down. Using her right, she grasped the rawhide tether. "Lolita, aren't you a lovely nanny?" She scratched the goat's forehead and cooed nonsense words but braced herself in case the goat tossed her head or bolted.

The young goats came close and sniffed then moved away.

"Hey, Hannah. Oh, excuse me."

Malin turned toward the door and had to glance downward to see the speaker.

A double amputee who held up his body weight on muscled arms ending in gloved hands filled the doorway.

Hannah straightened and patted the goat's flank. "No problem, Jimmy. What do you need?"

"Just letting you know a guy is out front with a couple of therapy dogs wanting to talk with you."

Therapy dogs? Malin's breath caught in her throat. *Tag's here?* She glanced toward the ranch manager to see if his arrival was planned or a surprise for her, as well. The raised eyebrows confirmed she wasn't expecting Tag. Could this meeting be a coincidence, or was he following her?

"Today must be the day for visitors." She strode toward the barn then paused in the doorway and tilted her head. "Coming, Malin?"

Remembering how she'd dashed out of the meeting at White Oak Ranch yesterday, she could only nod. Even after Hannah disappeared, Malin lingered, stroking a hand over the nanny's bristly coat. As soon as Tag proclaimed how she'd put her sisters in danger, she'd raced back to the ranch and made sure everything was all right—which proved to be the case.

Later, as she tossed and turned before falling asleep, she kept thinking about the stupidity of her behavior. The compelling man had only been looking out for her welfare. But she couldn't deny how every time he made a protective statement or gesture, she wanted to run into his brawny arms and let him keep her safe. She wasn't sure why, but she was willing to stave off the fear of men she didn't know well by whatever methods to spend more time together.

She trudged down the barn's main aisle, dreading coming face to face with Tag again. An apology formed in her mind. Her phone rang, and she grabbed it from her back pocket, glancing at an unknown number with an out-of-state area code. What was Caitlyn's code in Minnesota? She slid the pulsing bar. "Hello?"

"Malin. Rhys Morgan. Caitlyn said you asked about security at the ranch."

"I did. Thanks for returning my call." She slowed her steps.

"Only got a couple minutes to talk. I thought I told Tilda this info, but our departure to fly east was hectic. I left a case with a half dozen bugs and a small laptop in the bedroom shelf of the unit where you ladies stayed while I was there."

"In the overflow modular?"

"Right. Should I call Hank to send out his computer guy to set up and explain the program?"

Making sure more than just one person knew the system was a good idea. "That plan would be great." She'd reached the double doors and stopped in the shadows.

"But you know the surveillance being recorded needs to be monitored from the laptop itself. The system isn't the same as the type where silent alarms notify law enforcement of a perimeter breach."

Not exactly ideal. "I understand. Thanks, Rhys. Bye." She pocketed her phone and stepped into the sunshine outside the big structure. First, she checked the area for a black truck. Then, she directed her gaze straight toward the tall man standing near the corral fence but facing away from her position. His tight T-shirt and faded jeans looked like they were tailored for his muscled body. Her pulse ramped up.

When was the last time she'd been attracted to a man? Innocent flirtations with ranch guests didn't count. Had an entire year passed since Peter, the lawyer from Bozeman, and she drifted apart?

"Ah, there's the woman I mentioned." Hannah gave a beckoning wave.

Tag glanced over his shoulder then turned and grinned.

Her stomach spun like her favorite slot machine at Montana's Lil's Casino. No avoiding a conversation now. She covered the short distance with quick steps and glanced at the dogs sitting near Tag's boots, tails wagging in the scraggly grass. They were so cute. "Hello, Tag."

"Malin. Good to see you again."

"So, no introductions needed here." Eyebrows arched, Hannah glanced between them. "Tag's here to work his therapy dogs near the big animals. If you don't mind, Malin, will you take him back to the goat pen?" She pulled a walkie-talkie off a clip on her belt. "I need to check with Perry and see where he put the horses to graze."

"How are you—"

"I'm sorry about—" The collision of their words made her smile.

He dipped his chin. "Ladies first. Go ahead."

"I wanted to say that I appreciate what you and Hank said yesterday." She rubbed both hands down the front of her jeans then crossed her arms. "Running out so hastily was rude, and I really should apologize." She dropped her hands to her sides and offered a shrug. Why was she so nervous in his presence?

From under the brim of his straw hat, he stared with a narrowed gaze. "We only wanted you to know about the possibility. I never meant to scare you from the house." He stepped close and bent his knees so he was at eye level. "You seem tense. Are you all right now?"

The breeze brought her the scents of warm

male and a woodsy-sweet blend. Heaving a sigh, she shook her head. "If only you knew how many times someone asked me that exact question in the past month…" She jammed both hands on her hips and kicked her toe in the dirt. "I will be fine. Now, let me do as Hannah asked." She spun and stalked off toward the barn's doorway. "The goats are back here."

TAG GROUND his teeth and called himself six kinds of fool. Malin was the perfect case to benefit from what a therapy dog had to offer. He risked turning her off of the idea if he kept getting too personal. Seeing a desired target and going after it was ingrained. But he could learn to temper his attitude. "Pixie, Taffy, heel." He followed with long strides for about twenty feet into the structure. The scent of fresh straw and earthy leather teased his nose, and he inhaled. The smells always reminded him of home. "Wait, Malin."

She halted but faced toward the back of the barn.

He circled until he could see her expression. "Now, I need to apologize. For pushing too hard. For needing to know how you're feeling." If he touched her, would she jump back? He paused, silently urging her to tilt back her head so he could see her beautiful blue eyes. No question in his mind he needed that connection. For the past month, he'd thought of the way she'd looked to him for help during the robbery.

Her lips mashed together before she looked up. "Sometimes, your behavior ticks me off." She glanced to the side, chin quivering. "At others, I'm glad. Which, when you calculate the actual amount of time we've spent together, borders on a crazy thing to admit."

Hope warmed his heart, but he bit back a triumphant grin. "I don't believe that." He rested a palm on her shoulder and hoped she wouldn't shrug away. "And I don't think you do, either. Bonds created in times of crisis can be rock solid." The closing lines from one of his favorite movies, *Speed,* came to mind. He disagreed with Jack's warning to Annie that "Relationships based on intense experiences never work." But he liked her answer that she and Jack would "have to base it on sex then." A situation Tag definitely wanted to explore with Malin.

Malin sighed then dipped her forehead to rest against his chest. "Did what we went through that horrible day establish a bond? Is that why I can't stop thinking about you?"

"Could be." Closing his eyes, he relished her unexpected capitulation. The gesture was a small one but filled with a huge measure of trust. His blood pumped faster. He slid an arm around her shoulders and eased her against his body. "Or could be the fact that I'm a ruggedly handsome *and* all-around nice guy." He rested his chin on the top of her head and caught the scent of orange blossoms. *Lean on me, Malin.*

"Oh, really?" She laughed and clasped her hands at the sides of his waist.

He fought to ignore the sensation of her breasts rubbing high on his abs. The laugh was the first he'd heard, and he let the soft sound roll over his senses. The light-toned sound could signal she felt more relaxed in his company. "Sure, ask anyone with the last name of Redmond. They'll vouch for me."

"Small group of family members, is it?"

Her teasing was impossible to resist, and he bent down until only an inch separated their mouths. The heat from her rapid breathing fanned his chin.

Her eyes rounded, and she nibbled her lower lip.

The hold on his waist tightened as the gap between their faces narrowed. Fighting a pounding heart that urged him to claim what was within reach, he held himself back. Malin would be the one to make contact.

From somewhere, a goat bleated, and in the rafters, a bird flapped its wings then settled.

Focusing on other things kept him from wrapping both arms around her and tasting her pink lips.

Under a wrinkled brow, her blue-eyed gaze flicked between his eyes several times before she lowered her lids and stretched upward.

Butterflies landing on his skin would have exerted a more weighty touch.

A moan sounded. She slid her hands around to his back and grabbed handfuls of his shirt.

Yet, he stood still. Muscles locked on hold, he awaited the go signal. He told himself not to make a move until she committed fully to the kiss.

Her lips sucked at his, moving his lower lip between hers, then her mouth angled from the other direction. Fingers splayed wide, she grabbed his back.

Success. Tag released her shoulder and angled his arm downward to hold her tight. The firm muscles of her slim body filled his hand. He matched her pressure and molded his mouth against hers, doing his best to only mirror her nibbles and suckling to keep from going too far and scaring her. Even though what he wanted was to crush her body against his and dive deep into her luscious mouth. Warmth spread from every spot where their bodies touched. The blood surging to his groin warned him to pull back. But the sweetness of their connection was a mix of soothing and excitement wrapped together.

"What do you think Cookie's making?"

"Hope it'll be steaks. I could eat a two-inch slab of beef."

Male voices encroached on their magical moment. Tag moved in a circle to put his back toward the sound and eased away so they would have a chance to catch their breath. His pulse raced, and he watched Malin struggle to blink open her eyelids.

"Hey, who're you two?"

Tag glanced over his shoulder to see a pair of young men, each missing an arm, silhouetted in the open barn door. Guys must be veterans in the rehab program. "Friends of Hannah's. We're on our way to the goat pens." He shuffled Malin around to his right side then pressed a hand at her waist.

Cheeks glowing pink, she cleared her throat. "Yes, the pens are right outside the back door."

Still dazed by the effects of that kiss, he barely remembered to signal to the dogs before he followed Malin's lead. Then, he wondered when he could again get her alone and explore more of the spark they'd just ignited.

CHAPTER 5

GET your head out of your pants, Redmond. He had a task to complete and wondering about a sexy hook-up didn't fit on the agenda. Although he knew he'd be contemplating the possibilities later.

Tag glanced around the small fenced area and spotted four goats at the opposite side about thirty feet away. Contained space, big enough to stroll across and around. He might have to bathe the dogs when they got home, but the layout was workable. "My goal here is to walk Pixie and Taffy in the proximity of the goats but not be confrontational so they scatter." He grinned. "The pregnant nanny looks like she's not moving too quickly these days."

"I'm sorry, but I'm afraid I don't know much about therapy dogs. Other than seeing a news show or two about animals providing comfort in pediatric cancer wards or retirement homes."

"True on both accounts." He scooped up the dog with white-tipped ears. "Will you hold Pixie while I work with Taffy? Dealing with them both at the same time benefits no one."

Malin held out the back of her hand in front of Pixie's nose. "Hello there, girl. Remember me?" After the dog stopped sniffing, she stepped close to a tree-stump stool and brought the dog onto her lap. She ran a hand over Pixie's forehead then stroked a floppy ear.

Tag watched for a moment to make sure the pair was comfortable with one other then moved a few feet away. "In order to earn therapy certification, the dogs have to complete ten specific tasks. Because of where we live"—he spread out his hands, palms up, to encompass the ranch setting—"I like to also get the small dogs comfortable around large animals. That way, they're trained for all situations they might encounter in their new homes."

"Who are your target clients?"

He glanced her way and noticed Pixie lying in her lap while Malin stroked the dog's head. Malin's slim shoulders weren't so rigid, and her posture appeared more relaxed. "People like you."

Her eyes shot wide. "Me?"

"Yup, people who've experienced a major upheaval can really benefit." He decided to let her think on that. "Taffy, heel." He kept his strides short as he walked in a straight line toward the fence. To his left, the goats stayed in place but watched. "Taffy, haw." A foot or so from the fence, the pair turned left and walked the fence line. When he saw the goats sidestep or toss their heads, he changed direction, and then approached from another angle.

Taffy trotted at his side, seem unaffected by the presence of animals two feet taller and many pounds heavier. This easy-going dog had taken to his training program with gusto, and Tag was pleased with her progress. The reason he'd started them with medium-sized animals was because he knew goats were a breed with a fairly even-temper.

On each circuit, he glanced over toward Malin, who now leaned against the barn wall with her eyes closed. He walked close. "How are you doing?" Body language didn't lie, and he could see her previous tension had disappeared. Now, she needed to acknowledge the fact and recognize the reason why.

She shook her head and blinked fast. "What?"

"Tell me what you're feeling right now. Gut check and speak."

Her brows drew down into a tight wrinkle. "I think you're asking if I'm relaxed." She glanced upward and smiled. "Which I am. Almost like I've finished off a big glass of Moscato."

"What if you could have that feeling all the time?" Enjoying the sight of her lazy smile, he braced a shoulder again the fence rail.

"How?" Her eyes widened, and she tilted her head. "By becoming an assistant to your dog training program?"

An idea he hadn't considered. His pulse notched upward at the idea of having her around for that many hours a day. Normally a guy who shied away from a constant relationship, he noticed that knee-jerk negative reaction wasn't there. "No, I mean adopt one of these irresistible mutts. Training her through the final steps before the certification test would provide you with another focus."

"I don't know." She pursed her lips. "A pet's a big responsibility."

"What's the downside?" A horrible thought struck that made him take a step back-figuratively and literally. What if Malin didn't enjoy being around dogs the way he did? Had he ever been interested in a woman who wasn't a dog lover?

"Actually, while we were in Hank's office, I realized how much I missed having a dog in my life." Smiling, she ruffled Pixie's ears. "This little one slept on my foot."

Silently, he cheered. "Good to hear. Why don't you follow me home, and I can run you through a quick lesson?" The request was bold in light of their first encounter. But the kiss had gone a long way to knock down her earlier resistance. He lowered Pixie to the ground and lifted Taffy into her waiting hands.

She straightened and adjusted the dog on her lap. "I don't know."

He rested a hand on her shoulder, feeling her stiffen at his touch. Instead of backing off, he rubbed a thumb along the ridge of muscle, wrinkling the soft cotton fabric. That she didn't pull away encouraged him to press his luck. "The kennel isn't totally complete, but I'm proud of what I've accomplished in only a couple months. I'd like to show off the place." Under his stroking, her muscles relaxed, and he lifted his hand and moved to the side to put Pixie through the same exercise.

What he really wanted, no...what he needed...was to get a feel for how she'd fit in at the kennel—if she'd be intimidated by the noise and the activity, or if she'd dive in and help, like he hoped. The majority of his days were spent in canine company. Being around animals had always grounded him, and he wanted her to experience that same feeling and regain peace of mind. If he could be a part of restoring calm to her life, all the better. On a tangent where he walked facing her position, he saw her looking at her phone. Hopefully, she wasn't being pulled away.

"I have ninety minutes until I'm needed at the ranch to help with dinner preparations." She scratched under Taffy's chin. "Now, you've got me a bit curious."

Tag wanted to fist-bump the air. Instead, he took a steadying breath and held out his hand. "Let me put my address into your contacts." Although he didn't doubt she could find the place on her own, he made sure to keep her car in sight as he drove home. He needed the visual connection and didn't want to analyze why.

Anxious to get her working one on one with a dog, he kept the tour general and brief.

"What are the items in the backyard?"

"Agility work is a great tool for building rapport and trust between dogs and owners. These stations are the basic ones. Running through the activities make obeying the owner's instructions fun for the dog."

"Can you demonstrate?" She glanced over her shoulder and smiled. "I think seeing the interplay would help me understand."

That she was interested meant the first hurdle was passed. Malin wasn't dismissing the potential adoption out of hand. Tag handed her Taffy's leash. "Hold her, please, while I crate Pixie to keep her away from the action." He disappeared into another room for just a moment. Grabbing a hip sack with training treats, he secured it around his waist, and unclipped Taffy's leash.

Explaining each move as he worked Taffy on the equipment, he urged the dog through a solid tunnel, up one side of a steep ramp and down the other, wove through a set of six poles, and then up a ramp to a board raised four feet off the ground that she walked across and back down before jumping over two poles set at a one-foot height. He jogged Taffy back toward Malin, who grinned and applauded.

"That does look like fun. But I'll bet many training hours are involved."

Jazzed by her enthusiasm, he released Pixie from the crate and brought her close to Malin. "Because dogs love pleasing their owners, the training is not hard."

"Really?" She gestured toward the equipment. "Could you get us working together in the short time I have left here today?"

"Obviously not on all the apparatus." So far, he'd only trained Pixie on the weave poles. "But the tunnel's fairly easy."

"I'm not convinced any of these activities is easy." Malin shook her head. "Do you know how long our family dog took to learn how to shake hands?"

"I never teach that trick." He crossed his arms, glad to hear something personal about her background. "The dog gets nothing out of it." He waved a hand behind him. "With these agility moves, they have the chance to run and jump, activities which they love doing anyway. You're just channeling their natural energy."

"I definitely saw that in Taffy's attitude." Her eyes glowed, and she rubbed her hands together. "Okay, show me how."

He demonstrated the hand signals to put Pixie into a down and stay at one end of the tunnel and told Malin to walk around to the other end. "Now, crouch down and show her the treat you're holding."

Malin leaned over a little and held out her hand.

In that position, her body blocked most of the light coming through the opening. "Get lower. Pixie needs to see you down at her level." Tag moved behind her and brought his hands down on her shoulders to press her into the correct position.

Malin squealed and jumped to the side, wrapping both arms around her stomach. Keeping her head turned downward, she sucked in quick breaths.

The instant his hands made contact, he realized his mistake. The guy at the robbery had attacked her from behind, and that move must be a trigger. "Sorry." He forced calm into his voice. "Malin, I shouldn't have—"

"Don't apologize. The problem's mine." She

shook her head and looked up, her expression stiff. "I need to be going. Thanks for showing me your place." Then she turned and almost ran through the house.

Dullness coated her gaze again. Frustration burned a hole in his chest. He'd been playing off her enthusiasm and wanted to keep her excited about the process. *Damn.* He pounded a fist against his thigh. Why had he pushed like that? His action could be viewed as thoughtless and uncaring, when what he felt proved to be the exact opposite. Now, he could do nothing more than stand and watch her disappear. What if he'd blown any potential chance?

THE DRIVE HOME passed in a blur as she drove on auto-pilot. The act of stepping onto the ranch's garage floor made Malin realize she hadn't even checked her mirrors for the black truck. Fifteen minutes spent driving unaware of her surroundings because she'd been fretting over how she'd fled from Tag. *Stupid.* Shoulders slumped, she trudged from the garage to the back door, disgusted with her behavior. How were her actions those of a woman who captained her own life?

She yanked open the slider, glad to spot an empty dining room. Voices sounded from the kitchen, and she headed that way. Scents of herbs and roasting chicken wafted in the air. The rasp of a male voice made her pause in the doorway. Seeing her sisters standing behind a broad-shouldered, blond man seated at the kitchen built-in desk proved his trustworthiness. Even if his sheer size dwarfed the small area.

He pointed at various spots on the laptop screen. "Here's a wide angle shot of the front of the studio cabins. Where you three live, right?" He twisted to glance at Tilda, connected with Malin's gaze, and lifted a hand toward his forehead. "Hey."

"Oh, you're back." Jude skipped across the room and linked elbows. "Come meet Swede, who's a friend of Rhys. He's explaining where he put the camera do-hickeys Rhys left behind and how to operate the surveillance program."

"Hello, Swede. Sorry I interrupted, please continue." She stood several feet away as he demonstrated shifting the view from a single screen to one displaying four different locations on the property. Then he dragged the icon for the program that enabled listening in real-time onto the desktop. Because Swede talked her computer-related language, or possibly because he was part of the same company as Tag, Malin didn't experience any trepidation about the computer tech's presence. A positive step in the right direction.

"How long are the videos saved?" Tilda leaned a

shoulder against the wall to speak with Swede. "Or does the next day record over the previous one?"

To stifle a giggle, Malin pressed a hand to her mouth. Tilda might be a wiz in the kitchen, but her computer-tech awareness was a couple of decades old. Following Swede's instructions was easy, and Malin was confident she could handle any questions her sister had.

Twenty minutes later, he stood. "The program's a basic one."

Jude slid into the vacated chair and flipped through the screen views.

Tilda moved to the kitchen island and slipped on an apron. "Sure you won't stay for dinner? Seems like the least we can offer as thanks."

"Nah, I want to get home to Allie. She promised me lasagna tonight."

Malin looked up at the man who was about as tall as Tag but definitely more muscled. Interesting how everything came back to Tag. Malin walked him to the front door. "Thanks for your help, Swede. I'll sleep better tonight knowing the system is in place."

"Happy to oblige. Rhys might have only been in Montana for a short time, but he's still a part of Brotherhood Protectors. We'd do anything for one of our own."

"Good to know." That a cadre of well-built men —skilled in protective techniques and not afraid to face down trouble—were only a phone call away was a huge comfort.

He dug a set of car keys out of his jeans pocket. "I already sent my contact information to the ranch email address. Don't hesitate to call if anything goes wrong with the program." He lifted a hand and swaggered down the walkway into the waning sunlight.

After the meal cleanup was done, Malin begged off watching a DVD with her sisters. They'd drawn straws for the one who'd take the security laptop to her cabin on a rotating basis. Tonight was not Malin's night. Instead, she needed a long hot soak. The hot tub tempted, but she wanted privacy to figure out how to mend her friendship with Tag after her over-blown reaction to his touch.

More than once, she picked up the phone to contact Suzanne but never hit the icon to complete the call. Time to rely on her own methods for dealing with the stress. Instead, she created a relaxing atmosphere with scented candles, instrumental music, bath beads, and a glass of her favorite Moscato. As soon as the door was locked, she removed the clip and shook her head to loosen the crimped wad of hair. Bending at the waist, she scratched fingernails over her scalp then stood and tossed back her hair. Then she shed her clothes and stepped into the bubbly hot water. A heady vanilla musk scent wafted into her nose.

Fifteen minutes into her healing—both physically and psychologically—bath, she was as pliant as a well-cooked noodle. Watching the ends of her hair float on the surface of the water was mesmerizing. Then inspiration hit. She stretched for her phone and hit Tag's contact.

"Hey, Malin. Hang on." A cacophony of barks accompanied his abrupt statements.

The next thing she heard was a muffled thumping. Was that his heartbeat? Weird, but the sound created an emotional connection. As she waited with the phone pressed to her left ear, she dragged handfuls of fluffy bubbles over her chest. Silky water caressing her skin was pure luxury. Wouldn't having a certain someone close enough to scrub her back be the perfect indulgence?

Thoughts of what Tag's tight body might look like naked fueled her racing pulse. She'd heard members of the Brotherhood Protectors had all been injured during combat. Did his skin have many scars, or was his injury internal? Would his abdominals be defined into six or eight matching slabs? Her cheeks heated, and her nipples tightened. Only hours ago, she'd been pressed against his hard muscles, her softness melting against his steeliness.

Desire swirled in her belly. She captured the terrycloth washcloth, trailed it over her hip, and between her legs. She rubbed the rough cloth over her delicate folds, exciting her clit to erectness. Would Tag have cut marks in his muscles over the notches of his hips? Sensation built and zapped her nipples tighter. Arousal hit so fast her breath rasped through parted lips.

"No, that's too much. Only half a cup."

Oh shit! She froze, her body teetering on the cusp. Was he entertaining? Who was there at his house? Lost was her building orgasm. A stab of jealousy hitched her breathing. Maybe she shouldn't have called on impulse. With her free hand on the tub edge, she levered herself to sit upright. "What?" Her voice imitated a frog's croak.

"Sorry for the delay. A guy responded to my online ad for an assistant, and we got a late start on feeding."

"So, you already gave my possible position to someone else?" Where had she wrenched that teasing statement from?

Loud laughter carried through the phone line.

His laugh, deep and rich, wrapped around her senses and felt almost as comforting as being in his embrace. How she wished she was in the same room right at that moment. Were his eyes scrunched almost shut when he laughed? Did he throw back his head or hunch forward with a hand braced on a leg?

"Good one, Malin. But don't you realize that

hiring a kennel assistant is partly so I can see more of you?"

More of her? Although her blood heated, her reflex was to cover her breasts with an arm and glance around the room for hidden cameras. A reaction due to Swede's instruction on the surveillance system? Or had the wine sent her thoughts straight to sex? "See more of me, or see me more often?"

Three seconds of silence ensued followed by a throat clearing. "Uh, I vote for both, if being greedy is allowed."

The last few words were a sexy growl. Goose bumps rose on her skin. She needed to state the reason for her call before this conversation got out of her control. "Would you like to go horseback riding tomorrow or the next day?"

"Hell yes."

She grinned at his rapid response. "I'm available tomorrow after the weekend guests leave around two or anytime on Tuesday." Her words tumbled out so fast she sounded like an auctioneer.

He chuckled. "The earlier, the better. Tomorrow at two."

"Okay. See you then." She bit her lip. He'd decided so fast she couldn't think of anything more to say.

"Sweet dreams, Malin."

"Bye." Smiling, Malin set down the phone on the

bath mat then clasped chilled arms around her bent knees. Shivers attacked. The water had cooled during her phone call. As she climbed out and wrapped herself in an oversized towel, doubts settled in her thoughts. Would Tag think her invitation was only for a casual ride? Or would he recognize it as her shaky first step toward getting to know him better?

CHAPTER 6

WHAT MALIN WISHED for the previous night came true—her uninterrupted sleep proved thoroughly refreshing. Because of that, or probably because she'd see Tag today, she couldn't help smiling. Although both sisters gave her quizzical looks, Malin kept her secret to herself.

Today would be Tag's first chance to make an appearance at a pre-determined time. She wanted to be sure he fulfilled that implied promise before announcing the planned ride. Hopefully, he wouldn't act like her old boyfriend, Peter, who had often cancelled at the last minute and left her hanging.

As soon as she updated the website and checked for emailed reservations, she rushed out to the barn to groom two horses. Her favorite mare, Stormy, came right to the stall door and accepted the offered chunks of carrot. "Hello, Stormy. I hope one of the hands has been treating you right. I've been so busy I've been neglecting you." She lifted a hackamore over the gray's ears and settled the rope on her neck. "Today, we'll have a nice, long ride." Malin led Stormy from the stall, walked her across the barn's aisle, and slipped the end of the rope through an iron ring on a post. Then she went into the nearby tack room to grab the handle of the battered wooden crate filled with grooming tools.

After slipping on the curry comb, she circled it over Stormy's coat, working dirt and bits of straw to the surface. Then she grabbed a hard-bristled brush to scrape away the loose hair until the gray shined like pewter. "You're such a pretty girl. Don't these strokes feel so good?" The way the mare stood still through the procedure hinted at her pleasure for the attention. Using the softest brush in the box, Malin worked it over the face and legs with an extra-light touch. Saddling her and switching the hackamore for a bridle and bit took only a few minutes.

Then Malin repeated the process for Big Red. This roan gelding was the most recent horse brought onto the ranch. She hadn't worked much with the seventeen-hand high animal. Tag sounded like he had more experience around horses than she and could handle any of the gelding's bad habits. She stepped near the horse's shoulders.

"Hello, Big Red. You are a gorgeous animal. Look at the breadth of your chest."

With her right hand, she rubbed the comb in circles and followed with swipes of the stiff brush in her left. "Reminds me of a man I know." She ran the comb on both sides of the neck before moving to the roan's hindquarters. "Such fine muscle definition on your rump." Was complimenting a horse silly? Maybe, but she didn't care. Today, silly and carefree described her mood. She stretched on tiptoes to comb his back but had to duck into the tack room for a stepstool.

Once she climbed the steps and reached toward the horse's back, she spotted a silhouetted figure leaning against a stall. Recognizing the man's straw Stetson was the only reason for biting back her building scream. Then she remembered her comments and tossed a glare his way. "How long have you been standing there?"

"Can't remember exactly. Maybe since your comment about a broad chest"—he inhaled and squared his shoulders— "or maybe when you complimented the horse's tight rump." He turned and pulled his jeans tight across his rear, grinning over his shoulder. "See something familiar?"

Heat flamed her cheeks, but she couldn't deny she'd compared Tag's physique to the horse's. "Why doesn't that hat just pop right off your swelled head like a champagne cork?"

"No swelling of this head. Just hearing confirmation of the obvious facts." With long strides, he sauntered close. "Got a pick handy? I'll clean his hooves."

His outfit was one-hundred percent All-American cowboy from his denim shirt with the sleeves rolled back on his forearms to faded tight jeans and scuffed cowboy boots. If she stared any longer, drool might drip from her mouth. Shaking her head, she pointed the brush toward the grooming box. "In there. I always leave that task for last. Not my favorite."

"I can do the gray's, as well."

"Appreciate the offer." After quick strokes through his mane, she finished with the roan and returned the stool to the tack room. Then she took her turn at watching as Tag scraped out the horse's hooves and cupped his big hands around their joints, checking for the heat of inflammation. That he was thorough didn't surprise her. The realization sent her thoughts skittering to other activities where his attention might be just as diligent. Her pulse kicked into overdrive.

Without a task to focus on, Malin fretted about this ride. What would they talk about? Why had she even asked him along? Her original purpose had been for relaxation. Now, she doubted she'd draw a full breath until she watched his truck driving away at the end of the visit.

"All finished." Tag stood about five feet away, holding up the grooming box.

She blinked to focus then stretched out a hand. "Let me put that away, and we'll head out." Inside the tack room, she stole a couple of moments to brush her hands over stray wisps of hair and reposition the clip holding her hair at the nape of her neck. Then she grabbed her cowgirl hat and jammed it on her head. Turning and stepping forward, she almost plowed into Tag.

He held his position then slowly leaned down. "I wanted to say a proper hello." Tilting his head to avoid knocking off their hats, he brushed a light kiss across her lips then eased away.

His coffee-scented breath lingered. "Hello." The gesture was simple but oh so sweet. A thrill shivered through her.

Horse hoofs clumped down the middle aisle, and a dog dashed inside the tack room, tail wagging.

Tag huffed out a breath. "Barns used to be good places to sneak a kiss. At least, best as I can remember from my high school days."

Grateful for the distraction, Malin dropped to one knee and ruffled the fur on the Australian Shepherd's neck. Metal tags jingled together. She flipped one over and spotted a name. "Well, hi there, Barney. I don't think we've met."

"Is that you, Malin?"

She stood and glanced over at the dark-haired cowboy astride the buckskin called Biscuit. "Afternoon, Ryan. Is this your dog?"

"Yep." He waved a hand toward the horses. "Who's riding?"

Hoping her flushed cheeks had returned to normal, she moved through the door. "I'm going with my friend, Tag." She half-turned and gestured.

Tag followed and stepped to the horse to shake hands with the cowboy. "Tag Redmond."

"Ryan Fletcher."

"Malin, do you mind grabbing me a box of fencing nails? Since you're here, I won't have to dismount and tie up the horse."

She hurried to the back corner of the barn where those supplies were kept. As she jogged back, she tossed him the box. "We're riding along the creek probably as far as Rocky Point. I already told Tilda and Jude, but I thought someone down here should know, too." Then she vaulted into the saddle and headed for the door.

Tag joined her, and they walked into the warm afternoon sun together.

"Do you always tell a ranch hand your destination?" He tugged the hat brim a bit lower to block the slanted sunlight.

"We do. Luckily, that rule has been in place for as long as I can remember." Tag's mention of high school prompted a memory. "Probably initiated when my father realized his three teenage daughters were meeting boys at far-flung spots on the ranch."

"So, you didn't always use the barn?"

Laughing, she shook her head. "Almost never. Too many people coming and going." By now, they'd trotted a football- field length from the barn.

"That fact has been proven."

She clucked her tongue and tapped Stormy's sides with her boot heels. "Let's ride." The mare gathered speed beneath her. Malin caught the animal's rocking rhythm, leaning forward in the saddle. Spots of wildflower color mixed with the green prairie grass flashed into view then disappeared. She wished the meadow went on longer, but ahead, the trees of the Lewis and Clark National Forest loomed. Easing back on the reins, she murmured, "Take it slow, Stormy."

From behind came the hoof beats from Tag's approaching horse. "That was fun. You're a good rider."

She shifted in the saddle to look over her shoulder. "Been on a horse since I was twelve. Having any trouble keeping up?"

"I've got your six, Malin." His eyes narrowed before he smiled.

She'd seen enough movies to know what his military lingo meant. "Thanks." Malin guided Stormy into the shade and held her weight forward as the horse climbed the incline headed into the foothills. Keeping to the well-worn path through the trees, she didn't have to worry much about conversation topics. The surrounding beauty caught her attention, and she just enjoyed the view. With each passing moment, she felt the tension melt away.

Taking a spur trail, she guided them to a shallow snow-melt creek. Dismounting, she led Stormy to the water's edge for a drink. She grabbed a water bottle and finished half.

Tag crouched creekside and dipped his fingers in the rushing water. "Oh, that's cold."

She moved until she stood just a couple feet away. "Should be. It's from the peaks of the Rockies. But you must have similar creeks near your home."

"Not so close." He pulled off his hat and set it on the ground. "Our ranch is in the middle of a broad valley. But the summer grazing grounds have a creek." He scooped a handful of water and tossed it over his head then ran his fingers through his brown hair.

Droplets flung onto her shirt, and she gasped as the cold water penetrated to her warm skin.

"Uh, sorry."

"Yeah, right." Tipping her head to let her hat fall off backward, she scurried forward to grab water and toss the handful his way.

His head jerked back, and his mouth gaped.

Neither moved for several seconds. Then they sprang into action, straddled the narrow creek, and had a good, old-fashioned water fight.

After several minutes of play passed, Tag straightened and signaled for a time-out. "Truce." He jumped to the close side of the creek. "As fun as this was, I don't have a dry shirt or even a towel."

Malin ran her hands down her front, brushing away excess water.

"Oh, babe. Don't do that." Tag groaned and closed the distance until he stood a foot away. His dark gaze ran up and down her body.

Malin didn't have to look. She knew her cotton shirt was plastered to her curves like a second skin. The same way Tag's shirt clung to his well-defined torso. Unable to resist, she moved forward the last remaining inches and smoothed a hand over his chest. Already, the damp fabric warmed from his heat. Staying connected with his gaze, she stretched upward and licked a drop of water from his upper lip. A bit of beard stubble tickled the tip of her tongue.

He didn't move…he didn't even blink.

She rested her hands on his biceps and leaned close to taste his lips, pressing harder when she got no response. Had she misread the intent she thought his gaze held? Confused, she eased backward. "What's wrong?"

"Absolutely nothing. But I'm not making a mistake that will send you running." He sucked in a breath, his gaze searching hers. "That kiss felt too damn good to give you any reason to stop."

The backs of her eyes burned. That he considered her feelings meant so much. "That's sweet, but you're in front of me. I won't get surprised by your moves."

"As long as I go slowly, right?" A dark eyebrow slanted.

His teasing produced a grin. "Get out of my head, Tag, and kiss me."

After widening his stance in the gravel and dirt, he slipped his arms around her waist. "You good with this position?"

She nodded, lifting her face and waiting with anticipation.

He leaned down enough to brush his lips over her mouth then he drew back. "And that's okay, too?"

"I can see where this process is headed, and you're taking too long." She cupped her hands on his cheeks and pulled down his mouth so she could claim it, moving, questing, tasting, and suckling his lips until she drew out his response. *Finally.*

He took control and dipped his tongue inside, tangling with hers. Then he dropped light kisses along her jaw until he reached her neck and left a blazing trail to her ear and sucked her lobe into his mouth.

Malin clasped her hands around his neck, savoring the zaps of sensation skimming her skin. When he nipped her earlobe, she felt the tug deep in her belly. Her heart raced. A moan pushed its way through their fused mouths. Inside her damp bra, her nipples tightened, and she had to brush them against his rock-hard chest to intensify the sensation.

Seconds stretched into minutes. Or so they seemed to. She reveled in the strength of being held in the shelter of his arms, and she wanted the magic of their kisses to never end.

One of the horses shook its head enough to rattle the metal bit.

They both stilled then broke apart, but their gazes were constant. Tag clasped her hand and held tight. His breaths rasped.

That solitary disturbance reminded her she wasn't free to act with abandon. She still had to be aware of the unknown. True, the black truck couldn't follow them here. But if the robbers were locals, they knew how to ride. One look at the calm, grazing horses told her no other beings were nearby.

Without saying a word, he guided her over the creek and onto the top of a relatively flat boulder in the direct sunlight. She stretched out and tilted her face upwards, not caring that she'd neglected to apply sunscreen. The rock's warmth seeped through her clothes and warmed her chilled skin. As she lounged, letting nature dry her garments, she listened to the calls of birds and the chatter of chipmunks. Awareness of the sexy man who reclined at her side didn't allow her to totally relax, but she fast approached mellow.

One of Tag's fingertips traced circles around her knuckles and rubbed the ring she wore on her right hand. The gift from her parents for high school graduation—a moonstone surrounded by etched leaves set in a white gold band.

"Can I ask you something?"

"I guess." Asking to ask a question didn't seem like the topic would be fun. She mentally braced herself.

"Why do you wear your hair pinned tight? That day, the first thing I noticed was your long wavy hair in the breeze."

Blood pounded in her ears. She sat bolt upright. "Because my hair was used against me." After checking to make sure the clip was still in place, she jumped to her feet and turned toward the edge. Wearing her hair up was one change she'd made, and it comforted her.

Tag's boots scrambled on the rock, and he grabbed for her hand. "Don't run. Talk to me."

Suzanne warned her that the topic of the fear

about her hair would surface, and she'd have to face her feelings. Malin turned until she met Tag's gaze. "If I'd had short hair like Jude's, I might have gotten away." At the name, she saw his brows wrinkle. "One of my sisters."

"I don't believe that's the whole truth."

She yanked her hand from his. "How can you tell me what I feel? I know how the driver grabbed a handful of hair and pulled me into that truck. Wearing it down leaves me vulnerable."

He leaned forward. "My hair is short. Can you grab a handful?"

"Probably not." What was he trying to prove?

"Try it. Grab some and yank."

Was he making fun of her fear? "What you're suggesting is ridiculous."

He looked up, gaze narrowed and mouth pressed into a tight line. "I'm making a point. Humor me." Then he again looked toward the ground and waited.

Heaving out a sigh, she reached out and slid her fingers along his scalp then closed her hand into a fist and pulled.

He sucked in a breath and stepped in her direction. "Enough."

Immediately, she let go, cringing at the pained sound of that single word.

He straightened and rubbed his scalp. "Your grip forced me to move."

"But I felt your hair slipping through my fingers. I couldn't have pulled you off your feet."

"Besides the fact I outweigh you by at least sixty pounds." After a final rub of his head, he braced both hands on his hips.

"There's that." She touched the clip to double-check it held tight. "The length of my hair is a detriment to my safety, and I can't allow it to be used as a weapon again."

"Why not cut it short and relieve yourself of one fear?"

"Really?" Since high school, she'd always worn her hair long. Plus her mom used to cut it and since her passing, Malin only went to the salon for occasional trims. "Do you think my fear would go away?" Could reducing her anxiety be as easy as making a trip to the salon?

"My philosophy is if you see a problem, you figure out a way to solve it." He shrugged. "This solution could be one way to get rid of that problem."

Excitement at the possibility raced along her skin. Could the solution really be that easy? "Let's ride down this mountain and get to town." She scrambled off the boulder and jumped the creek.

"Wait, Malin. I have one request."

With her foot settled in the stirrup, she glanced over her shoulder. "What?"

"Remove the clip and let me touch your hair." His chest rose and fell, and his gaze darkened.

Turning, she reached for the clip then shook her head as she watched him approach. His intensity was daunting. More than six feet of hard muscles bore down on her. Could she move past her fear and let herself be vulnerable? If she didn't trust him, then she would never have suggested this horseback ride. She unclasped the clip and tilted her head until she felt the length unroll down her back. Giddiness fluttered in her chest. When he skimmed his fingers through her hair, she shivered and closed her eyes.

TAG DIDN'T KNOW when he'd last trembled like he did now at the idea of touching Malin's hair. He'd heard somewhere that allowing a person to touch your head involved a high level of trust. With gentle strokes, he slipped his fingers against her temples then moved farther along her scalp. The faint scent of orange blossoms accompanied his moves.

What started as a simple request to create a tactile memory for when her hair was gone turned into an act more sensual than he'd imagined. He filled his palms with the soft strands and let the tendrils flow over his fingers. Blood rushed to his groin, and he fought to ignore the sensation.

Stepping close, he nuzzled his nose at the top of her head, and silky strands caught in his short whiskers. With every move, he became more entangled with Malin. He glanced at her face, seeing how she'd closed her eyes and that a corner of her mouth quirked upward. Why the hell had he suggested she cut it off?

At the selfish thought, he moved his hands back to his sides and spread his stance to ease the ache behind his jeans fly. "Thanks for indulging my request." He watched her eyelids flutter a couple times before they fully opened.

"Uh, sure." She turned toward the gray horse, wobbling a bit.

An hour later, he stood opposite of where Malin sat in the first chair of three in the hair salon. She'd chosen not to face the mirror. He vowed he'd be her rock so she wouldn't falter in this decision. The entire drive from the ranch she'd chattered about upcoming guest events, the weather, and apparently any other topic that crossed her mind. He understood this decision was a big one. But he couldn't forget the huge sigh of relief she'd expelled when she proclaimed this haircut was what she wanted. His job was to see that the change actually happened.

The stylist set a picture book in Malin's lap.

"Sure you don't want me to snip off just two or three inches?" She flipped a few pages then pointed with the comb. "Like this one?"

Malin didn't look down, but she shook her head. "Cut it a bit below my earlobes, Regina." She set the heel of her hand against her neck. "Right here." Then she looked up and met his gaze.

He nodded and flashed a smile to show his encouragement.

Frowning, Regina twisted a comb in her hand. "As long as I've worked here, you've only asked for a trim. Like twice a year."

Tag crossed his arms over his chest, a posture he knew intimidated. "Do as Malin asks."

Regina startled and glanced over her shoulder, eyes widening. "All right." She reached for a water spray bottle and started squirting.

When the first long strand hit the floor, he glanced at the curled shape, masking his internal wince. But with every snip afterward, he never looked away from her blue-eyed gaze. Malin sat like she'd become a block of ice. Her expression was so stiff he couldn't tell what she was thinking... or if she took many breaths.

Finally, Regina stepped back. "It's done. Do you want a bit of gel or mousse? Or do you want me to swivel around the chair so you can see?"

"M-mousse." Her gaze flicked to Regina then

reconnected with his. The knuckles on her hands gripping the chair arm whitened.

That's it, Malin. Own the change. In silent support, he dipped his chin. Now, he felt nerves attacking his gut, because he wanted her reaction to be positive. He watched Regina work white foam through the short strands then finger fluff them until waves caressed Malin's cheeks.

"Okay, Malin. The moment of truth is here." Regina depressed the silver bar at the base of the chair to lower the height then she grasped the back and walked the chair around in a half circle.

Gasping, Malin lifted her hands, bouncing her palms under the cut ends. Then she tilted her head from side to side. A smile grew on her mouth. "Regina, wipe that worried look from your face. I like it."

For the first time in thirty minutes, Tag shifted position and dropped his hands to his sides, flexing his fingers.

Malin stood and turned, her eyes wide.

His admiring grin was her answer. He reached into his hip pocket for his wallet. "My treat." As soon as Malin stepped toward the door, he stooped near the chair, grabbed a foot-long tendril of honey-blonde hair, and tucked it in his jean's pocket.

The woman with the jaunty step he followed out of the salon was not the same woman who'd walked inside. He stepped to where she'd stopped on the sidewalk and scanned the area for any black trucks. "Where to next?"

She turned and linked her hand into the crook of his elbow. "I want you to teach me a few self-defense moves."

Just who had he encouraged to step into the light of day?

CHAPTER 7

MALIN LAUGHED at Tag's wide-eyed expression. "Come on, don't look so shocked. If I'd known self defense, couldn't I have avoided what happened at the bank?"

He stopped and grabbed both her arms. His thick eyebrows crashed downward. "Don't think like that. You should never oppose anyone holding a gun, especially not when the weapon is pointed at your head."

Pinned by his dark-eyed gaze, she sobered, her stomach reeling like a pinwheel. "But you were ready to go against them."

"I'm combat-trained, you're not."

Crossing her arms, she frowned, hoping hers looked as determined as his did. "Exactly my point."

Huffing out a breath, Tag looked off into the distance.

She wondered if he knew he rubbed his hands from her shoulder to her elbows as he thought. Not that she was complaining, because his rough hands felt good anywhere on her body. The realization should have shocked her. A week ago, the thought would have prompted a panicked call to Suzanne. Instead, Malin allowed it to settle deep inside. *I really care for this protective man.* He was like no guy she'd ever dated. In almost no time at all, he'd become an important presence in her life.

"Don't the residents of Eagle Rock miss having a gym?" Tag slid his hand under hers where it clasped her left arm. "Let's head back to your place. The hayloft is as good a spot as any to do some throws." Then he turned and walked toward his truck, tugging her behind. As he moved, he scanned the parking lot and road.

"Throws?" Glad he'd agreed, she was unsure about the sound of what he planned. When he'd pulled the truck into traffic, she angled her body to face him. "Shouldn't I start with smaller moves like wrist bending or foot stomping?"

"Who's the expert here?"

"You, but…"

At the next stop sign, he glanced sideways, eyebrow cocked.

She knew he didn't intend that look to be downright sexy, but her pulse kicked up anyway. "All right, you're the expert. Don't you think we're a bit unmatched weight-wise? You even pointed out how much bigger you are than me."

"And you need self-defense moves because only a person who is your same size will be the attacker?"

"Well, no." Why did he have to be so logical? She rested her elbow on the window frame and watched the familiar scenery pass. What she wished for was never to be attacked again…in her entire lifetime. But she also didn't want to experience the helplessness of that day. As she rode, she tilted her head and felt the ends of her hair tickle her neck. This new style would take some getting used to.

Tag parked the truck near the barn, and they both hopped out. He met her at the front of the truck and reached for her hands. "Promise me that if at any time you get freaked, you'll tell me to stop."

Now, she was confused. "But I'm the one who asked you to teach me."

"Right, but some of the moves are responses to attacks from behind. Can you handle that situation?"

From behind was her trigger. She bit her lower lip. "Since I know we're practicing, I think I can."

"Let's do it." He released her hands and waved her to go ahead.

Malin walked to the wooden two-by-fours nailed to the barn wall leading to the hayloft. She had almost reached the top when a hand wrapped around her ankle. She gasped, and her stomach clenched in a knot. Then, she looked over her shoulder and took a calming breath at the sight of a familiar face.

"Now, jerk your leg in any direction to break my hold. Go for it."

The first two sideways attempts failed, but on the third, she bent her knee and yanked up her foot, breaking his grip.

"Good move."

As she climbed to the loft, she figured he probably let her win that one. For the next twenty minutes, she listened to everything he said and learned about stances, weight distribution, and leverage. Mostly, she'd attempt to break a hold only to have Tag remain standing followed by him correcting her posture or the placement of her hands. Twice, she succeeded with a leg sweep so they both tumbled into the loose hay. Moves that earned her a wide grin and high-five from her handsome instructor. Her confidence grew. Plus, she had the added bonus of being held close.

An alarm sounded, and Tag reached for his back pocket.

Malin straightened and swiped a palm across her perspiring forehead, shoving damp tendrils to the side. "Problem?"

"No. A reminder about a meeting at Brother-hood Protectors."

"You should go." For the past several hours, they'd been together in an isolated bubble—with only one another for company. If she didn't count Regina. Even then, Malin had been laser-focused on Tag's gaze. But she couldn't steal all his time.

"I want to find out if Hank's heard from Rayburn." Frowning, he glanced between her and the phone. "But what we're doing here is important, too."

She lifted a shoulder and let it drop. Bits of hay tickled at her neck and down her back. Now that she'd stopped moving, she realized how itchy her skin was. "So, come back tomorrow."

After pocketing his phone, he stepped close and cupped his hands at the nape of her neck. "That's a given." He leaned down and captured her mouth for a quick, but thorough, kiss.

Hot and powerful, the kiss sizzled, and she grabbed onto his ribs for balance. The tang of their sweat mingled with the fresh scent of straw, making a heady combination. Way too soon, Tag stepped back, releasing her.

"Gotta go." He lifted a hand close to her fore-head and flicked away a piece of straw.

"I know." She mirrored his action and pinched a long blade that was caught in his thick hair.

"I like the new do." A thumb caressed her lower

lip before he turned and disappeared down the ladder. "Talk to you later."

"Bye." She stepped to the edge of the loft and watched him stride from the barn before she climbed the ladder with slow steps. As she moved, twinges erupted along her sides where she'd strained to lever him over her hip. Maybe what she needed was a real self-defense course taught in a gym with cushy mats. If she located one nearby, she'd insist her sisters attend, too.

On the walk to the main house, she untucked her blouse and pulled the tails away from her body, releasing some of the hay bits. No guests sat on the deck as she crossed, her boots clunking on the wooden planks. The reflection in the slider showed where straw dotted her much-shorter hair. How had Tag chosen the single one he removed? She shook her head then stopped. A shower would solve the problem.

Malin walked inside and nodded at the couple sitting in one of the couches. She headed for the kitchen, counting on running into Tilda. But the room stood empty. A glance at the clock confirmed this was meal prep time. Then she remembered today was Monday and Tilda's quasi-day off. She still prepared meals, but guests on Mondays and Tuesday were served reheated leftovers from the weekend menu.

Malin walked to the main foyer and listened for

sounds from anywhere in the house. Music floated down the stairs, and she followed the notes to the library/media room, pausing in the doorway. Bookcases lined one wall with two Queen Anne-style chairs facing the filled bookshelves. A Tiffanyesque stained glass pole lamp stood between. Overstuffed couches sat on three tiers and faced a huge television screen. Currently running was an action movie Malin had sat through several viewings with Tilda. An interruption shouldn't cause an issue. She wondered what reaction she'd receive about her shorter hair. Taking a breath, she stepped into the room. "I'm back."

"Uh, huh." From her perch in the top row, Tilda didn't take her gaze from the screen.

Malin walked across the room and plopped into the corner of the lowest couch. This car chase involving backwards driving was always exciting, and she settled in to watch. When it ended, the image stilled.

"You cut your hair!"

"Yep." Smiling, Malin turned and giggled at Tilda's look of total amazement. "I talked out my fear of how its length made me vulnerable."

"So, Suzanne suggested the change?"

"Nope, Tag did."

"The guy from the robbery who I still haven't met, but I heard rode Big Red today?"

Strange that so much had happened in the past couple of days that strengthened her relationship with Tag, but she hadn't yet brought him into the main house. What was her reason for not introducing the three most important people in her life? *Oh, Malin, quit analyzing every choice and decision.* "I'll check when we can do introductions. But do you like the new style?" She stood and turned her head to show off her profile from both angles.

"Very complimentary."

"Think of how easy it will be to maintain." She ran her splayed fingers through it and came away with several pieces of straw. "Yuck, I've got to shower."

"Is that hay you're dumping on the carpet?" Tilda leaned forward.

"Tag showed me some self-defense moves in the barn." She wriggled her fingers in the air. "I'm off to shower. Call if you need help with getting dinner on the table." As she headed toward her cabin, she wondered if she'd run into Jude first or if Tilda would share about her haircut. Amazing how one simple change lightened her step and lifted her spirits. She slid the key from her front pocket and opened the door.

An unknown scent slid past her then dissipated before she could identify it. Maybe she needed to check her mini-fridge for expired yogurt. After dropping the key in the ceramic bowl near the door, she headed toward the bedroom but slowed. The novel she'd started reading last night had been on her nightstand but now lay in the middle of her couch. She scanned the room and spotted several items in places where she knew she hadn't left them. The hairs on her arms rose.

Even though they'd been apart less than an hour, she grabbed her phone and called Tag, hoping to hear him say she must be imagining the disruption. Better, that he would be right over to assess the situation. That answer was the one she wanted to hear most of all.

Hand shaking, she leaned a shoulder against the wall, "Tag, I need you."

TAG LOUNGED at one end of a couch in the living room of Hank's White Oak Ranch. Four other agents showed up for the meeting—Swede, Taz, Bear, and Mad Dog. He wondered at the number of years of skill and experience held by the assembled six men. All located in this out-of-the-way spot in rural Montana.

Hank started at four o'clock with the announcement of another new agent due within the month.

That produced nods and grunts of acceptance around the room.

Turning his gaze toward Tag, he extended a

piece of paper. "I received that first thing this morning. You're officially on the clock for guarding Malin Langstrom."

Tag glanced at the photocopy of a five-thousand-dollar check from a bank in St. Paul, Minnesota. "Isn't St. Paul where Rhys is living now?"

"True, but the payor isn't the same as the one covering the work related to Caitlyn Auliffe." He shrugged. "Could be the same benefactor, but all I know is the money's in our account."

With a nod, Tag set the paper on the nearest table. Disappointment ate at his gut. The check changed things—he had to figure out to what extent. Their relationship had been advancing in the right direction, but now he was officially on the job. As much as he hated the idea, he might have to pull back from his romantic pursuit. "Hear anything from Rayburn?"

"Only that the BOLO is still in effect, but no responses." Hank turned to Taz. "What's your update?"

Tag doubted a successful result from a "be on the lookout" report on a truck with only a paint color as the distinguishing feature. The reports from the other agents floated around his awareness as he contemplated what could be his next steps to find the suspect's truck. He needed a new strategy. A loud throat clearing disrupted his musings.

"What?" He glanced around and discovered he was the focus of everyone's attention.

"Anything else to report?"

"Not at this time." He straightened. "I've got to figure out a new resource for locating that truck."

Hank stood. "Meeting's over. Appreciate you all showing up."

The agents cleared the room in a flash. And Hank walked toward his office.

Tag grabbed the photocopy from the table and followed. "You need this copy for your files?"

Hank extended a hand to collect the paper. "You figured out an angle for sticking close to Malin? Is she still in denial about the presence of a possible threat?"

"Uh, about that." Tag slumped into one of the visitor chairs.

Hank leaned a hand on the side of his desk. "The last thing I want is to get into your personal business, Tag. When you and Malin met in my office, did I sense something more than a friend-ship going on? Sadie tells me I'm oblivious some-times, so correct me if I'm wrong."

"Not exactly. But I'm not ready to label what's going on. All I know is the lady is hot and funny but vulnerable as hell." Listing her attributes produced the image of her relaxed, smiling face to mind. A warm feeling settled in his chest. "Being honest, boss, we've shared a few kisses but nothing more."

"Crap, I hate discussing this topic." Hank rubbed the back of his neck then moved to sit in his chair.

A horrible thought blocked out everything else, and Tag sat forward, elbows on knees. "If the company has a stated hands-off policy, then..."

A snort sounded as Hank shook his head. He leaned back in the chair and clasped his hand behind his head. "Look at the Brotherhood Protectors' track record. If I'd instituted a hands-off policy, it's been overlooked by just about every agent, including myself. Distance, both physical and emotional, is hard to maintain when situations get intense. I've lived that experience. What I ask is gentlemanly consideration. Or the best that a Ranger can give."

The older man's wide grin added a teasing note to the jibe. Tag snapped a salute. "Rangers lead the way, sir." While on active duty he'd seen rivalry when Special Forces from various branches served on the same assignment. But not since coming to Eagle Rock and sitting around the living room at the meetings. Agents represented a mix of decorated ex-military—Delta Force, Rangers, Seals, and a bounty hunter or two—but in their civilian roles, they pulled together as one.

"Wise ass."

"Count on it."

His phone vibrated, and he grabbed it. The caller ID named Malin. He'd have to snap a picture to add to her contact record. "Speaking of whom…" He lifted a finger to put a hold on his conversation with Hank. "Hey, Malin. I didn't expect—" Hearing her whispered words "I need you" stiffened his posture. He narrowed his gaze on a knot in the wood flooring so he could listen to her trembling tone. "Where are you? What's happened?"

Her response sounded rushed and stuttered at the same time. He lifted his head and met Hank's gaze. "What I understand is you think your cabin's been broken into? No, I'm sure you're not imagining it." Damn, why hadn't he taken ten minutes and done a check of the property's layout? Without the situational survey, he couldn't visualize her cabin's location in relation to the entrance or the main house. Driving to the barn guided him down a road away from the main property. "Go to the main house and don't touch anything in your cabin. I'm on my way." He punched off the call. "You heard what's going on?"

"I'll contact Joe Barron." Hank rested a hand on the desk phone. "You'll stay there until a deputy arrives?"

Tag gave a curt nod. Anxious to get to her, he jingled his keys in his hand. "I don't think inventing an excuse to stay close will be necessary." He turned to leave, his thoughts already with what Malin was going through. *Damn.* She'd looked so happy when he'd left Dream Vistas.

"Couldn't tell if you heard the details, but Swede set up motion-detector units on the property's perimeter and connected the surveillance program. He gave the sisters instructions yesterday, so ask to see the footage."

"Will do."

"Because of the rural location, the settings are high so a deer or raccoon doesn't set off the recording. You might have to adjust those."

Tag waved a hand over his head on the way out. "If I get stuck, I'll call Swede." The next ten minutes elapsed in a flash of trailing clouds on dirt roads and passing slow-moving vehicles on the asphalt. He left the truck in the ranch's circular drive and ran up to the porch.

A slender woman with light blonde hair opened the door and stood in the foot of open space. "Yes?" Squinting, she looked him up and down. "You're Malin's Tag."

"I am. Where is she?" Pulse beating double-time, he stretched to see past her spiky hair.

"Tag!" Malin stepped into the long hallway.

Relief shot through him at seeing her. He narrowed his gaze on the door guardian until she stepped back to let him pass. "Any other problems since we talked?"

She just shook her head.

As he moved toward her, he glanced around at the layout of the huge house and up the staircase. Too many damn access points. Great for entertaining… suck-city for protection. He dragged off his hat and tossed it on a nearby chair then enveloped Malin in his arms. A few seconds passed as he rested his chin on the top of her head and breathed in her familiar orangey scent. "You'll be fine, babe. I'm here."

"I'm glad." She nestled closer.

From this position, he could gauge her state of mind. Her voice sounded steadier than on the phone, and her hands weren't shaking against his back. "Hanks says you have security footage. I need to see it." He eased away but kept an arm around her shoulders.

The woman who answered the door stepped ahead. "Through here."

Tag walked with Malin, supporting her more than following.

Two women stood at a kitchen island, facing the doorway.

For expediency sake, he took charge of the dialogue. "Tag Redmond from Brotherhood Protectors. I'm assuming you two are Malin's sisters. Show me the surveillance footage."

Malin rounded the island and pointed toward the blondest woman. "My younger sister, Jude, and that's Tilda."

"Thank you for coming." The older one spoke then pointed toward the built-in desk.

Nodding his acknowledgement to the introductions, he crossed the room and slipped into the chair. After checking the program's name, he hit a few keys and watched the screen for a change in the gray-and-white images.

At sixteen thirteen, a human-sized blob moved from one side to the other at the bottom range of security camera number five. Then it disappeared. Tag fast-forwarded until the recording reached the current time, and the screen grayed again. To gather every shred of info, he re-ran the footage twice more.

A brimmed hat obscured facial features. The person hadn't lingered near any objects that would help to gauge his or her size. "Who knows the location of camera five? I want to see the spot."

Silence.

He turned to where the women huddled together around the island. They looked at each other and shrugged.

"Swede did the set-up." Jude leaned toward the island and set her chin in her raised fist.

Malin approached. "He didn't show us where he put the cameras. We figured the position would be obvious from what displayed." She waved a hand toward the laptop. "But now I see that assumption was wrong."

A knock rapped on the front door.

Malin jumped.

"Relax, babe." He stood. "Hank called the sheriff to investigate. That's probably him."

"He did what?" Tilda shot to her feet, wringing her hands. "Mr. Redmond, we have guests here who don't need to be upset by a law enforcement presence."

"Miss Langstrom." Tag fought to remain civil. "Your sister has a stalker who means her harm. In my book, that threat trumps your guests' peace of mind." Before he dug himself any deeper with Malin's sisters, he strode to the front door and stepped outside. "I'm Tag Redmond from Brotherhood Protectors. I believe my boss made the report." He extended a hand.

"Sheriff Joe Barron." The big man returned the handshake. "You're assigned to one of the Langstrom sisters?"

Having the sheriff familiar with the security company helped speed the process. He nodded. "Malin."

"Where was the break-in?"

"At a studio cabin. I was just about to learn which one."

The sheriff jerked his head toward the closed door. "May I go inside and speak with the ladies?"

Tag cleared his throat. "The oldest sister is concerned about upsetting the guests. How circumspect can the situation be handled?" There, he'd done what he could to appease Tilda.

"If a guest gets curious, I can inquire about an available weekend for a family reunion."

"Great."

"Not my first rodeo, Redmond." Barron stepped forward and entered the house.

The sarcasm stung his ears. All right, so maybe he was being a bit zealous because of the target's identity. How could he get Malin to agree to come to his house? For her own safety, she needed to be away from this location. At least until surveillance was beefed up. He let the sheriff handle gaining entry to the correct studio while he signaled Malin to a corner of the kitchen. "How are you doing?"

"Can't deny I'm rattled." Frowning, she bit her lower lip. "Someone was in my house and touched my things." A shudder ran through her body.

Needing to touch her, he rested a hand on her shoulder. "I need to check the cabin. Will you stay here, or do you want to go along?"

She placed a hand on his chest. "I want to stick with you."

Minutes later, after Deputy Meadows shot

photos of the entire place, Tag stood in the doorway to the bathroom, out of the way.

Malin walked through her living space, which measured fifteen by twenty. She pointed out items that were in the wrong places.

Meadows slid each item into a plastic evidence bag and made notes on the label.

The studio was well-built and efficient. Open living space included a galley kitchen, round dining table with four chairs, couch, an armchair, and three-shelf bookcase. Stairs along one wall led up to a sleeping loft. Thankfully, the longer she worked the process with the crime scene specialist, the calmer she appeared.

His phone chimed, and he glanced down at the screen displaying an out-of-state phone number. Finger poised over the off button, he looked again and recognized a San Antonio area code. Stepping inside the bathroom, he toed the door mostly closed. "Tag Redmond."

"Is this MWD handler Redmond?"

Tag leaned a hip against the sink. The voice was vaguely familiar, but he had too much going on to place it exactly. "Former. Medically discharged six months ago."

"Tag, this is Master Sergeant Hernandez at Lackland Air Force Base."

Lackland was the site of the training school for dog handlers from all military divisions. "I remember being in your class. What can I do for you, Master Sergeant?"

"We just processed an injured dog here I think you know. Dex sustained a broken leg on his last assignment."

"Dex?" His favorite. His gut clamped tight, and his hand gripped harder. "How's he doing?"

"Not great. The break is close to the hip, and the recovery will be long. His file is stamped medically unfit."

Not a good prognosis. Tag winced. Here was a wrong he knew he could make right.

"I'm contacting previous handlers to see if adoption is a possibility or desirable."

"Hell yes, I'll adopt." Tag's injury was what broke up the team, and the feeling he'd deserted Dex had bothered him every day since his military separation. "Is he fit to fly?"

"Not advised. You know how commercial lines treat big dogs. The largest crate will be hard for Dex to move in because of the length of his cast. Plus the weather issue. You've lived in south Texas. Temps are already in the eighties here."

"Crap." Tag ran a hand though his hair. "I live in Montana now." He thought back to the trip he'd made to the ranch from Lackland after he finished training. "The drive is at least thirty-six hours one way, and that estimate includes only four or five hours of sleep."

"Can you get someone to share the drive? Sorry, Redmond, but I need a confirmed arrival date and time, or I contact the next name on the list. You rated the first call because you and Dex served as a team the longest."

Details raced through his mind. He couldn't drive *and* tend Dex if the dog needed attention. Could Tag get the new kennel assistant to move into the house for several days? Yanking open the door, he drilled Malin with a stare.

At that sudden movement, she looked up, eyes widening. "What?"

"No worries, Master Sergeant. Give me forty-eight hours to pick him up. Don't let anyone else adopt him." Tag ended the call. "Pack a bag. We're taking a road trip."

Malin walked close, her gaze searching his. "What are you talking about?"

"Would you rather stay in Eagle Rock and possibly come face to face with your stalker or be safely away from here for a few days?" What he didn't say was she'd be stuck inside his truck for the majority of that time. Explanations came later, probably accompanied by apologies.

The adoption was something he had to follow through on. He would not fail Dex a second time.

CHAPTER 8

MALIN STARED AHEAD at the dark highway broken only by the SUV's headlights and shifted her grip on the steering wheel. The prospect of a road trip with Tag had sounded fun—even though convincing her sisters involved more backbone than she usually displayed. Through all the hours of conversation, they could get to know each other really well. And she suggested they drive through Yellowstone Park. Both suggestions were met with a cocked eyebrow and total silence.

A little less than eight hours into the trip and already she doubted her decision. Her idea of a road trip included sightseeing stops and actually sitting in a restaurant to eat, instead of juggling fast-food while behind the wheel. Not so for this dictatorial man who mapped out the most direct route and insisted they were young and healthy and could drive straight through. Thirty hours of driving! At least, when they'd stopped at his house for his go bag, she convinced him to bring along Pixie. The simple act of leaving the state didn't cancel her moments of panic. She lowered her hand to rest on the dog's head that warmed a small part of her right thigh.

One thing Tag said was true. She glanced sideways toward his body slumped against the passenger window, blanket pulled under his chin. They were certainly far away from any chance of being stalked.

Blinking away the grittiness of tired eyes, she focused on the road. Every once in a while, a grouping of trees broke up the monotony of asphalt and painted lines. Probably the view of the high prairie would be beautiful during daylight hours. The last big city she'd driven through was Casper. The destination for switching drivers was about halfway between Casper and Cheyenne. A glance at the dashboard indicated less than forty minutes remained in her four-hour shift.

Not wanting the radio to disturb Tag's rest, she had to entertain herself. What had she learned about Tag so far? He liked onion rings on his burger and preferred root beer to cola. When music played, he chose classical country stations. He didn't snore. In fact, he hardly moved while he slept. After they'd switched drivers at Lodge Grass, he hadn't stayed awake long enough to snap her picture next to the Wyoming state sign—one of her childhood family traditions that she carried on when she could. Maybe she could catch it on the way back. Oh jeez, had he done a similar rundown on her personal traits during his driving shift?

The sign announcing her destination made her perk up. She glanced longingly at the tall billboards advertising major chain motels and bit back a sigh.

Tag awoke the moment she braked for the off-ramp marked with the fuel symbol. He stretched and scrubbed his hands over his face. Then he reached across the console to run a finger on her shoulder. "How are you feeling?"

"It's almost four in the morning so the answer is tired." Ooh, that statement was snappish. She wrinkled her nose and glanced his way. "Sorry."

"No problem." Leaning forward, he looked around then pointed to the left. "That gas station looks open. Is this Douglas?"

"Aye, aye, captain. I fulfilled my mission." *I really need to grab some sleep.* She depressed the left blinker and steered toward a small convenience store/gas station with glaring overhead lights. After waiting for Pixie to potty in the vacant lot next door and giving her water, Malin stumbled into the convenience store and used the facilities. Already, she and Tag had a routine. She tended Pixie and bought the road-trip snacks, and he dealt with whatever the car needed at that point.

Hank deemed the trip Brotherhood Protector business because of Dex's future potential as an explosive-scent-trained dog and authorized use of a large company SUV. She looked forward to stretching out on the backseat. After her nap, the cities blurred together, and she spotted names she'd never heard of--Eads, Lamar, Campo, Etter.

One place that made an impact was a rest area near Stratford, Texas, where Tag agreed to pull over and nap together for a glorious three hours. The back of the SUV wasn't anything fancy or soft, but the vehicle hadn't been moving. Sleeping in Tag's strong arms created such security that she enjoyed solid rest.

Bright light battered at her eyelids. Moaning, she threw up a hand. She'd purposely slept with her head toward the east so the door blocked the rising sun.

"You awake back there?"

How was he so chipper? Her whole body felt grungy after minimal cleanups in gas station bathrooms. Balancing on the toilet seat to change clothes when she could no longer stand her own stink hadn't been fun...or easy. The car curved into a wide circular turn, and she grabbed the armrest. "Where are we?"

Pixie yipped and slid off the seat into the foot well.

Malin petted her until the dog settled again then she sat up so she could catch Tag's gaze in the rearview mirror.

"Central Texas."

The same answer as hours ago when she'd last asked. She glanced at the clock and saw he'd driven past his normal stint. "Why didn't you wake me?"

"Because I was planning a surprise." He braked for a red light then turned. "Come up here."

With awkward moves, she climbed over the console, avoiding a watchful dog and cup holders. As soon as she sat, she fluffed her sleep-flattened hair into a semblance of presentable. This style took almost no care at all. Why hadn't she cut it years ago? "Okay, I'm listening. What surprise?" A glance around showed surroundings that included more than green rolling prairie. She spotted buildings.

"Highway construction farther south forced me to deviate from the planned route. We're headed into the Hill Country, which I've heard is scenic."

Malin leaned forward, wide awake now as they rolled through a small town just opening up artsy tourist shops and setting out chalkboard signs on the sidewalks. Anything other than two-lane divided highway looked wonderful. "Thanks, Tag." Her smile grew as they passed a city park along a creek where a group performed a Tai Chi devotion. She spotted joggers under huge shade trees and people watering front lawns. Nice to know everyday life went on.

Tag kept checking the phone balanced on his thigh. He navigated a series of turns moving away from the small town's busy street. Then he pulled to a stop in the parking lot of what looked like a motel.

Sucking in a breath, she wanted to look at everything at once. Mostly, she focused on the sign with the word "resort" in the name—a label that meant a hot shower and a bed. "Don't tease me. Are we staying?"

"We're a bit ahead of schedule. You've been a relatively good sport and deserved a treat."

She snorted. "Love the qualifier, Redmond."

"Well, you're not the easiest person to wake up."

"I'm used to more than three hours of sleep at a time. Call me a wuss." Malin unlocked her seatbelt and jumped out of the vehicle. "Hurry up. I've got dibs on the first shower."

Tag must have been busy while she slept, because within ten minutes, they were registered and inside their room that boasted everything western. Wagon wheel headboard and lampshade, wooden horse sculptures on the wall, and a bath mat in the shape of Texas. Mountains, horses, and teepee decorated the bedspread.

This room was smaller than one at a national chain motel, but she labeled it cozy. As she luxuriated on the fresh sheets wearing a clean sleep shirt, she listened to the running water on the other side of the wall. Her pulse thrummed with building anticipation. Eyes closed, she imagined soapy rivulets traveling over his muscled shoulders and down across his pecs. Would the trails slow their descent through his chest hair? Did he have much body hair?

Then she didn't have to wonder because he stood next to the footboard made from a tree branch, bark and all. A small patch of dark hair shadowed the cleft of his pecs and narrowed to a trail that disappeared beneath the towel wrapping his hips. In this case, the reality was better than the fantasy, and she aimed to discover everything about the ex-soldier before her.

"I wish the shower stall was bigger."

Interpretation: I wanted to be naked with you under the steamy water and help you wash. Her throat dried. He'd already asked her twice if she was all right with sharing the room. "Did you set the alarm?"

He nodded, his gaze roaming her exposed legs.

At some point during one of her driving stints, she'd decided this trip was the perfect opportunity for them to explore their sexual compatibility. Not that she had doubts they'd be good together...her racing heart proved that fact. Here in this out-of-the-way place, they were just another anonymous couple.

No one from Eagle Rock would see a vehicle parked at the other's house and ask questions. He wouldn't have to tiptoe out of her cabin, hoping not to run into a sister or a ranch hand. The door was locked, Pixie lay in her crate, and the next six-and-a-half hours were theirs to spend how they wished. Grinning, she crooked her finger.

Tag crawled across the mattress then lowered his head and shook off the excess water.

Perfect tension breaker. Giggling, she grabbed him around the neck and pulled him across her chest, kissing her way up his neck. He'd shaved, and the sweet-woodsy scent of his cologne filled her nose.

His hand slipped under the hem of her shirt and inched upward.

Malin caressed his shoulder, tracing the line of his clavicle, but very aware of his hand approaching her breast. Her pulse skittered, and she told herself to relax.

He cupped the small mound and paused. "How's this? Am I rushing you?"

Turning her head, she looked into his deep brown eyes. "I see you, Tag, and I can smell your scent. I'm not afraid. Only nervous."

"Nervous? Why?" His hand massaged as he spoke.

She arched into his touch, feeling her nipple pebble against his palm. "Because a while has passed since I've done...since I've gone to bed..." Him rolling her nipple between his fingers stole her words.

He tweaked a finger tip against the end of the tight peak.

Pleasure sparked. She lost her train of thought and stifled a moan against his hard chest.

His response was to toss the towel over his shoulder and strip off her shirt. Then they stroked and caressed, nibbled and licked, discovering secret erotic spots, as well as ticklish areas. Her stomach clenched when she saw the puckered skin on his left thigh, and she arched an eyebrow.

He shook his head. "Another time."

Taking turns, they laid still while the other explored the feel and taste of napes and elbows, insteps and backs of knees. She learned the small of her back was sensitive to hot breaths. He groaned when she massaged the muscles at the base of his skull. Small pleasures that developed trust and intimacy.

By the time she could no longer ignore her shortened breaths or his rigid erection, she was comfortable with touching and being touched. Positioning herself on her side facing him, she reached out to stroke his steely length, trailing her fingers along the veins and circling the edge of the mushroom cap-like.

Tag caressed a palm over the rise of her hip and down her leg to her knee before skimming upward along her inner thigh.

A memory flashed from that awful day of multiple hands groping. She tensed.

"Malin, open your eyes. You're safe."

She did and looked into his steady brown eyes, pinched at the corners. "Right. I'm with you, and I'm safe."

"Good, now can you release my cock?" His words whooshed through gritted teeth.

Gasping, she opened her hand and glanced down to see white stripes becoming pink again. "Sorry." A finger pressed against her lips.

"No need to apologize. We'll figure out what works and what doesn't." He rubbed circles on her hip. For several moments, he moved his hand closer to her pussy from different angles.

But no matter if his touch was light or heavy or fast or slow, every time she tensed. To distract herself, she repeated the motions on his body, watching his arousal grow from the flush darkening his cheeks to the tight cords in his neck as he fought against giving in. She wanted to share in that excitement. The very fact Tag was being so patient and focused on her needs endeared him. Except neither was actually getting off. A state she really hoped she be closer to by this point. "Maybe foreplay won't work this first time. Maybe I need quick penetration to break through the impasse in my mind."

"You sound so clinical. Are you sure?" His brows lowered, but he rolled to the side and dug a hand into his bag. Then he moved to sit on the edge of the mattress to shuffle through the clothes.

"Blame my therapist, Suzanne. She warned me the first time might be challenging." Blowing out a breath, she flopped back on the bed. "Obviously, what we're trying isn't working."

Tag glanced over his shoulder. "Are you slamming my abilities?"

"Not my goal, but frustration makes me witchy."

"Not touching that comment." He leaned down again.

The play of muscles as he twisted and reached caught her attention. She ran a fingertip below his shoulder blade and encountered a raised scar. "What's that one from?"

"Shrapnel."

Intellectually, she'd known as a soldier he'd been in combat. But seeing the evidence of an injury hurt her heart. "And your thigh."

"Bigger piece."

Pushing upward to her knees, she stretched to kiss the bump. Then she slid a hand under his arm and around to his chest, circling a finger around his puckered nipple. Rubbing her breasts against his back-shot zings of arousal to her core.

"Damn, that feels good, babe. But I can't touch you." He reached a hand over his shoulder and cradled the back of her head.

"That's okay. For now." She moved her hand from nipple to nipple in counterpoint to rubbing herself on his bulged muscles. Her skin heated, and her heartbeat pulsed in her nether lips. Flexing her hips, she pressed harder. "Sit against the headboard."

"Gimme a second." He dropped his hand from her head. A rip sounded then a moment or two later he rolled to his back, fully sheathed.

Malin didn't hesitate to straddle his hips and brace her hands on his shoulders. "I need to do this at my own speed."

"Let me kiss you first then I promise hands off." He stretched upward and molded his mouth over hers, battering with nipping teeth and probing tongue then retreating to gentle brushes.

Malin accepted every dive of his tongue and circled hers around his. She ran her hands along his neck and cupped his cheeks so she could slant her mouth in a different direction. Desire hit in her core, and dewy juices wet her channel. Barely able to breathe, she whimpered when the heat disappeared. Wow, and only his mouth had touched her. What would a full advance involving hands, body, and legs feel like?

She centered her pussy over his rigid shaft and eased herself downward. His girth stretched her moist lips, and the burn ramped up her excitement. Making little bounces, she moved her hips lower to accept more of his cock.

Tag reached for her then dropped both hands to the sheets and gripped with his fists. "You're so tight, babe. Feels amazing."

Flexing her hips created perfect alignment. Giving shallow thrusts, she rocked in that one spot, alternating with slow circles to rub her clit against his coarse groin hair. Needs hit all at once, stalling her arousal. Her channel was filled to the max and needed release. Beaded nipples ached for friction so she fell forward against his chest, rubbing through the bristly hairs. The movement dulled the pressure on her G-spot.

Frustration wrenched a sob from deep in her throat. Grabbing the branch above Tag's head, she levered herself up and down the length of his cock.

"Let me help, babe."

"I don't know how." She rocked, but penetration alone wasn't enough. Her gaze locked on his.

His jaw clenched as he curled upright until his arms braced his torso only inches away.

Greedily, she ran her nipples up and down against his wall of chest muscles as she regained her hip flex rhythm. The dual stimulation revved her pulse, but her arousal plateaued. "Tag," she rasped. "I need your touch."

"Where?"

"Nipples, breast." Her breaths panted from her open mouth.

His eyes flared, and he grinned as he bent closer until he caught her jiggling left breast between his lips and sucked in a mouthful. His tongue stroked the underside.

Malin inhaled, reminding herself the woodsy scent belonged to Tag, the man who cared about how she felt and allowed her to set the boundaries.

Her flexing quickened, thigh muscles screaming with the extended strain. When a pinch centered on her left breast, she squealed then stilled before her body jerked. Orgasmic pulses flowed through her and sent twitches to her other muscles. She slumped forward, draping her arms over Tag's shoulders.

He released her breast and kissed his way to her ear. "Can I hold your hips?"

Limp as a rag doll, she could only nod.

Strong hand cupped her hips to keep her in place as he thrust upward in long strokes alternating with circling ones. Harsh breaths grunted from his throat as the pace increased.

Malin revived enough to plant her hands next to his thighs and flex into his last few thrusts.

Then he arched his back and held tight while his cock emptied. A long release of air sounded before his body relaxed backward.

On shaky limbs, she moved off his hips and tumbled against his hot body. The last thing she remembered was expelling a satisfied sigh and cuddling into Tag's strong embrace.

CHAPTER 9

THE BLARE of a trumpeted reveille disturbed Tag's dream of entwined limbs, the heady scent of arousal, and a body relaxed from hot sex. When he grabbed for his phone to silence the alarm, he realized he hadn't been dreaming.

With a sleepy protest, Malin patted a hand over the mattress until it encountered his ribs then she sighed.

That soft sound went straight to his heart. Even in her sleep, she sought the security of physical touch. Last night's lovemaking proved to be both the most challenging and the most soulful he'd ever had. Watching her work through her demons in order to share intimacy, without his active participation, tested his own self-control. Hearing her plea and seeing her quick response to his touch strengthened his feelings for this brave woman.

Once the room was quiet again, he gathered her close and closed his eyes. Just five more minutes.

From the other side of the bed, an alarm bonged like a church bell.

Malin sat upright and squinted in all directions, searching the immediate surroundings with patting motions. "Where's my damn purse?"

Tag settled a hand behind his head and watched her fumble to locate and silence the church bells. Years in the military had trained him to function on reduced sleep at various times of the day or night. But his sweet lady must need a minimum of eight, and all during the darkness. He'd witnessed her bumbling her way through the first several minutes after each awakening. Not the most sexy of sights.

Tempted as he was to feel her naked body nestled against his, he had a deadline to meet. And they had a ninety-minute drive to reach Lackland, possibly two hours if traffic was heavy. Spotting Malin curl again into the fetal position prompted him to jostle the mattress.

"I'm up." She lifted her head and glared in his direction through tousled strands that covered her eyes.

"You showering?" He retrieved the towel off the floor and knotted it around his hips.

"Sure, but you go first and warm up the room."

He pressed a hand to the window and scoffed.

"Malin, we're in Texas, not Montana. Temperature is in the mid-eighties."

She adjusted her cheek on top of her clasped hands. "Then you make the coffee, and I'll get up."

That one was a new delaying tactic. "Picking up coffee from a drive-thru."

"What?" She shot upright on braced arms. "We're not eating in the resort's restaurant? I looked forward to ordering a meal from an actual menu I can hold in my hands."

Winking, he pointed. "Gotcha. Bet your blood's pumping now. We're leaving at fifteen hundred hours." Now that things were settled, at least in his mind, between him and Malin, he could focus on Dex. The return trip didn't have a hard deadline so they could play the schedule by ear.

Two hours later, they crawled along the 410 Loop at twenty-five miles an hour. On a four-lane divided freeway, five lanes in some places. He'd forgotten that frustrating fact about this sprawling city of a million and a half residents.

"Have you ever seen so much traffic? Where is everyone going?"

"Home. After four o'clock is commuter traffic." At least, today wasn't Friday.

"But we're almost to the base, right?"

He glanced sideways and saw her stretching toward the back seat to reach Pixie's paw. "Less than twenty miles. Malin, Pixie can ride with her harness clipped to your seat belt."

"But the front seat's not the safest place for her. I'm fine." She faced front again. "Are you excited about seeing your dog again? Want to talk about your feelings?"

"After that session earlier today, I'm all talked out. In fact, I've never heard so much talking during sex." He was quick to rub a hand over her knee. "Just teasing, babe. I'm glad you worked through what kept you trapped." All of a sudden, the congestion loosened and their speed hit forty-five, quickly closing the distance on their destination. He started looking for the correct exit. Now that Malin mentioned feelings, he recognized signs of tension—the base of his skull was tight and he kept flexing his fingers around the steering wheel. Him being cool and relaxed at the human-canine reconciliation offered the best chance to re-establish their prior relationship.

Thirty minutes later, Tag needn't have worried. From the moment he rounded the back corner on the row of kennel runs, he heard Dex's welcoming bark. "I'm coming, Dex." Pulse pounding, he broke into a jog, scanning the runs until he spotted the brown-and-black dog with the point missing on his left ear. War wound. His gut clamped tight. "Hey, buddy. I'm right here."

Sometime later, that's where Malin found him—

sitting on a concrete slab with Dex's head in his lap, running his fingers through the Malinois's thick coat. His grateful tears had dried, but he didn't care if she spotted any remaining evidence.

Being with his buddy and knowing a good place waited in Montana healed the worry he'd grappled with for so many months. Dex and he were a team again. Within a few weeks, they could get back into training.

"Tag, are you all right?" She grabbed hold of the chain link fence and lowered to a squat. Her gaze searched his face.

Pixie sat on her left side, panting.

Dex crawled forward to touch noses with the Beagle through the fencing.

"Hey, that's my line. We're fine, just reconnecting."

A frown wrinkled her brow. "You left the SUV almost an hour ago."

"An hour, really? Sorry, babe. I hope you didn't feel abandoned." He pushed to a stand and brushed dog hair off his clothes. "Guess I better find the kennel master on duty and get the adoption paperwork signed."

THEY SPREAD the return trip over the bulk of three days, including deviations from major highways to allow for sightseeing. Cell service proved reliable enough for keeping in touch with their respective businesses. The easier driving pace allowed for long conversations about their childhoods and hopes and dreams for their futures. Tag determined stopping in motels would give Dex's leg a rest from the vehicle jolting. A side benefit was two nights of romping sex exploration that left Malin and him sweaty and satisfied.

Only a few hours from home, Tag's phone rang. Still hadn't bought the hands-free device. That task would be a priority. He reached over from the driver's seat to the console, swiped the screen, and tapped Speaker. "Redmond."

"Tag, Detective Rayburn. Do you know where Malin Langstrom is?"

The harried tone in the man's voice brought Tag to full attention. He shot a sideways glance and met her surprised gaze. "Right beside me."

"And you're where?"

"Driving out the north entrance of Yellowstone at Gardiner headed toward Eagle Rock." He braked for a steep downhill curve and hoped the signal didn't cut out this far below the ridgeline of the Rocky Mountains.

"We think we've located the black king-cab."

"Where?" He cut a sideways glance toward Malin.

"Abandoned in Lewis and Clark Caverns State

Park with a busted axle. Looks like someone tried driving in the forest."

Malin grabbed his forearm. "That's not far from Dream Vistas."

He nodded. "Appreciate the update, Detective."

"If any matches are found, I'm expecting a fingerprint report sometime tonight. I've put a rush on the results."

"Roger that. Keep us apprised of anything else." He tapped the red button.

"Should we warn Tilda and Jude?" Malin lifted her phone from her lap.

He stretched across the space then rested their linked hands on the console. "And tell them what? We don't know enough yet to get them worried. The sheriff is conducting nightly stops, Swede's monitoring the system, and Hank had guys doing walk-throughs of the grounds a couple of times while we've been gone."

"You're right. But as we drive closer to home, I can feel the tension returning. Up until that phone call, I saw you checking the rearview mirrors more than usual."

Damn. He thought he'd been subtle. "Only a few times. But now we can relax. The truck's bound to reveal fingerprints. If the last two are like the first suspects, they have records."

They stopped in Livingston for burgers and to switch drivers. But neither had much of an appetite and ending up feeding the meat to the dogs. Just as Malin turned into the Dream Vistas' driveway, Tag got a call, leaving Malin to unharness the dogs.

Tag put the call on hold and lifted Dex out of the SUV then went back to his call.

The device that held up Dex's hindquarters laid at the back of storage area. Malin wrestled to lift it out.

But Dex walk-hopped on three legs to the corner of the garage then laid down. After glancing over his shoulder and whimpering, he struggled upward and moved along the building before dropping again.

Malin waved an arm and pointed. "Tag, what is Dex doing? I tried to lead him to a tree, but he's over by the garage."

TAG DISCONNECTED the phone call and watched. When Dex repeated the motion, Tag tensed and turned toward Malin. "How many times has he done that?"

"The last was his third. What does it mean?"

"Dex is a scent dog, and he's picked up a trail." Needing to hide his growing concern, he stepped in front of her and hugged her tight. "Love you, babe, but I need to get to work. Grab Pixie and hightail into the house. Call Hank and tell him to send in backup and get his best bomb tech over here."

"Bomb?" Her eyes rounded.

"Go, Malin. Now." At the back of the SUV, he shoved aside their bags of clothes and souvenirs and opened the hatch. Thank God, Hank was an organized guy. Tag pulled out a Kevlar vest and a hard hat and strapped them both on. From a small compact box, he pulled an earbud and inserted it-- just in case the device was still set to the right frequency. He sorted through the other vests until he found the smallest size and rushed to fasten it around Dex. With leash clipped tight to Dex's collar, Tag waited for the dog to struggle upright then gave the command. "Seek, Dex, seek." He wished like hell he had a handgun, but his KA-BAR would have to suffice.

With no waver in his path, Dex set off in a straight line from the back of the garage across the open field. Four more times, he dropped to a lying position and held it.

"Good job, Dex." Tag dropped flat to the grass. The line was clear, and Tag sighted on specific trees to get the bearings straight. "Time to wait for rein-forcements, buddy." Tag rolled to his back and told his body to relax. Early in his career, when he had the need to prove himself, he would have tracked the scent into the forest alone until it ran out.

But, the older and wiser Tag Redmond had

someone to live for and a beloved's feelings to consider before he ran off playing at being a solitary hero.

A hand nestled deep in Dex's fur, he stared at cloud formations until a click sounded in the earbud.

"Redmond, you on this line?"

"Reading you, Hank."

"You slacking off, Ranger?"

"Who's asking?"

"Taz, on your three o'clock about nine hundred out."

"Mad Dog on your nine, north side of the barn."

"Patterson on the road in a whirlybird standing by. Waiting on your go, Redmond."

Tag rolled to his stomach and used his scope to locate the other agents. "Have your bomb tech check the garage. Dex marked spots along the west side."

"On the move."

Tag made one last reading and signaled for Dex to stay.

Dex whimpered and made crawling motions with his front paws.

Tag held his collar tight and stared into Dex's eyes. Then he gave the abrupt, flattened-hand signal again. As much as Dex had already helped, on the uneven terrain, he'd only slow Tag's pace. Rising to a crouch, he took two deep breaths. "Go, go, go." In a bent position, he jogged to the tree line and looked for a foot trail. Whoever put the explosives in the garage probably left the property in this direction.

Mad Dog and Taz converged on his location and joined the search. The men walked three abreast with heads angled downward.

"Bear here. Working downhill from Rocky Point. Headed toward a red tent near a flat boulder beside a creek."

The memory of the water fight with Malin surfaced, but Tag pushed it aside.

Mad Dog straightened. "Need back-up?"

"Going solo."

Minutes passed with only the crunch of leaves as the men looked for footprints.

Taking too long. Hairs on the back of Tag's neck rose. Something was off.

"Tent's empty. But I found rope and a floor plan of a multi-story house."

"Shit, it's a diversion. Get back to the main house." Tag spun and ran hard, dodging under branches and around trees. "Possible abduction in progress."

"Taz, approach from the back." Hank gave command instructions. "Mad Dog, swing around to the front. Report when you breach and helo will block the driveway. Tag, be cool. The tangos are not leaving the property."

As the men moved into position, no one reported. Tag broke from the trees and spotted an empty field. No Dex. Running in a zig-zag pattern toward the deck, he heard Taz hot on his heels.

Remembering a tall shade tree, he headed left toward the spa. In no time he'd scaled enough branches to drop onto the roof and gain access through an upstairs window. Too many accesses paid off in his favor. He unsheathed his knife and crept down the hallway, clearing each room he passed. A video played in one room with the volume muted. He left it running.

At the head of the stairs, he heard the murmur of voices, all female. Had the agents returned before the kidnapper made his move? Somehow, taking a different path in the forest? Reaching the bottom stair, he heard a scratch on the front door and pressed himself against the entry wall, knife raised to shoulder height.

The door eased open, and a tall form, clothed in camo, stepped inside.

Mad Dog. Tag waited until the ex-soldier made eye contact before signaling a forward direction then right turn. Why did they women sound so calm? Tag hesitated just short of the doorway and dropped to his knees. He pulled a telescoping mirror from a vest pocket and scoped out the kitchen from floor level.

Two of the kitchen chairs held bound and gagged men.

What the hell? Tag jumped to his feet and stepped into the room, sweeping his gaze around but not finding Malin. He took a moment to glare at the scumbags who'd caused his love such heartache.

A whoosh of the sliding door off the back deck sounded followed by gasps.

Tag crossed the floor in long strides until he saw the back of Malin's head then he slowed.

"Don't be alarmed. Brotherhood Protectors, ladies."

Tag waved a hand. "Taz, all clear. Two tangos are immobilized and breathing."

"You're back." Malin jumped up from her chair, clasping Pixie to her chest.

Dex whined from under the table, his long tail thumping the floor.

"How you'd accomplish the capture?"

"Swede called about seeing movement on the surveillance monitor. So we gathered the available resources." Malin circled her arm to include the group. "Pixie sounded an alarm. Jude had pepper spray. Dex blocked the front door. I didn't want to get close enough for a hip throw, so I just used the always reliable kick to the balls." She grinned, her eyes flashing.

Tilda patted a hand on an antique rifle lying on

the table. "Didn't hurt that I had our granddaddy's sawed-off shotgun for backup."

He glanced at the ex-soldiers who just stared and busted out a laugh. Seems their skilled and coordinated tactics were upstaged by loyal canines and resourceful women.

EPILOGUE

A MONTH LATER, Malin waited with Pixie and about twenty other human-canine pairs to complete therapy dog certification. Tag sat somewhere in the bleachers of the Bozeman Auditorium. But she was too nervous to look his way.

Her world had changed so much. She enjoyed mingling with Dream Vistas guests again and had no fear when approached by a stranger in public. Dex's cast was now shorter to give him use of his knee joint so he walked with an almost normal gait. She and Pixie proved to be a good match, and Malin was convinced they'd bonded on the road trip. She put the dog through her paces for three hours a week to train on the essential ten tasks. Best of all, she and Tag spent as much of their free time together as possible.

Hearing her name, she stood, signaled to Pixie,

and walked toward the evaluator. A low level of nerves kept her on her toes, and she started off Pixie like usual. The Beagle trotted at Malin's side and performed each task with precision. When they were done, she searched for Tag who punched a victory fist into the air.

Dex sat at his side, pink tongue lolling from his mouth.

Waiting through the rest of the examinations tested her patience. But her reward came in the form of a gold embossed certificate. Better was the hug and toe-curling kiss from Tag.

Grinning, he held her at arm's length. "I knew the first time you looked at Pixie that a match was meant to be. Nothing can beat the loyalty of a furry companion."

"Except maybe the loyalty of a Ranger." She sealed her statement with a kiss, knowing that although she'd never be a Ranger, her loyalty and love were tied to the strong man in her arms.

ALSO BY LAYLA CHASE

Ranger in Charge, a Brotherhood Protectors novella

Historical releases

Her Captured Cowboy in *Cowboy Heat,* an anthology

The Maiden's Kiss in *Hot Highlanders and Wild Knights,* an anthology

Paranormal Releases

Ghostly Legacy in *Masters of Desire,* a 3-author anthology

Contemporary Releases

Heated Negotiation

Hot for the Uniform

Naughty in Norway

Naughty in Norway also found in *Destination Pleasure,* a 9-author anthology

On An Escort's Arm

Setting Boundaries

Up and Coming

Twin Delights

Wanton Words

Whirlwind

Challenges Met in *Blue Collar,* a Boys Behaving Badly

Anthology

All authors appreciate hearing how their artistic creations are received by readers. With so many titles available, standing out from the crowd takes a bit of extra effort. I would humbly appreciate you spending a few moments to give your honest opinion of this title by going either to the book page on Amazon or Goodreads and listing a short review.

ABOUT LAYLA CHASE

On a dare from a close friend, Layla Chase challenged herself to explore the steamier side of romance and discovered characters whose stories needed sharing. She writes contemporary and historical stories about strong personalities who know what they want...or rather, **who** they want, and set out to get it.

To connect with Layla on the web:

Website
www.laylachase.com

Facebook
http://www.facebook.com/layla.chase.52

Amazon
https://www.amazon.com/author/laylachase

f facebook.com/layla.chase.52

a amazon.com/author/laylachase

ORIGINAL BROTHERHOOD
PROTECTORS SERIES

BY ELLE JAMES

Brotherhood Protectors Series

Montana SEAL (#1)

Bride Protector SEAL (#2)

Montana D-Force (#3)

Cowboy D-Force (#4)

Montana Ranger (#5)

Montana Dog Soldier (#6)

Montana SEAL Daddy (#7)

Montana Ranger's Wedding Vow (#8)

Montana SEAL Undercover Daddy (#9)

Cape Code SEAL Rescue (#10)

Montana SEAL Friendly Fire (#11)

Montana SEAL's Bride (#12) TBD

Montana Rescue

Hot SEAL, Salty Dog

ABOUT ELLE JAMES

ELLE JAMES also writing as MYLA JACKSON is a *New York Times* and *USA Today* Bestselling author of books including cowboys, intrigues and paranormal adventures that keep her readers on the edges of their seats. With over eighty works in a variety of sub-genres and lengths she has published with Harlequin, Samhain, Ellora's Cave, Kensington, Cleis Press, and Avon. When she's not at her computer, she's traveling, snow skiing, boating, or riding her ATV, dreaming up new stories. Learn more about Elle James at www.ellejames.com

Website | Facebook | Twitter | GoodReads | Newsletter | BookBub | Amazon

Follow Elle!
www.ellejames.com
ellejames@ellejames.com

facebook.com/ellejamesauthor
twitter.com/ElleJamesAuthor